A Mystery Inside

A NOVEL

By Sunny Reilly

How a 92-year-old author
takes on bullying
and secrets
with the help of friends,
letters and Angels

Dear Bully

Dear Mom and Dad

Dear Friend

outskirtspress

DENVER, COLORADO

A Mystery Inside
How a 92-year-old author takes on bullying and secrets with the help of friends, letters and Angels
All Rights Reserved.
Copyright © 2013 Sunny Reilly
v2.0

Cover Photo © Janine M. Torsiello. All rights reserved - used with permission.
Back Cover Author Photo © George M. Aronson. All rights reserved - used with permission.

Outskirts Press, Inc.
http://www.outskirtspress.com

ISBN: 978-1-4787-1089-9

Library of Congress Control Number: 2013911619

Outskirts Press and the "OP" logo are trademarks belonging to Outskirts Press, Inc.

PRINTED IN THE UNITED STATES OF AMERICA

ACKNOWLEDGEMENTS

In gathering material for this book, I've discovered many earthly and heavenly Angels. I believe there are some heavenly Angels that know me, but I don't really know them. I just know they are there and available if I need them.

Then there are people in my life who have become my Angels. Some of them are still here and in my life every day – just like Sara. Others have been here in my life but have become heavenly Angels – like my Roger. They were here, now they are gone. But they are never really gone from me. All of these Angels I write about in this book.

I am grateful for these Angels and for the following people who helped make this book a reality: In particular, I'd like to thank Janine M. Torsiello, my good friend, who edited this book, encouraged me and held my hand on this journey. In addition, many thanks to Gail Rudder Kent, Connie Stober and Michael Giuliano, members of The Writer's Club at the Park Avenue Club in Florham Park, NJ, and especially the many earthly and Heavenly Angels of my "family" at the Morristown Unitarian Fellowship.

You know who you are – because all you special Angels made me do it.

Sunny

CHAPTER 1

ANGELS WANT GIGI TO MAKE AN ANNOUNCEMENT

GiGi glanced at the clock. It was only 9 a.m. but her Angels had been tugging her to make the announcement. It did feel like an announcement kind of day. It was sunny and the air was crisp. It was still too early to call her friend Sara since they usually called each other after 10 a.m.

Actually her name was Gillian Graham but everyone called her GiGi. She liked it better that way for a number of reasons but mostly because it was a twist on grandmother or great-grandmother. It was something that had started a long time ago with Sara's girls, but at 92 years old she had picked up a lot of little ones and not-so-little ones along the way who learned to love her and call her GiGi. She and Sara both had a way of picking up strays. Sometimes it got her into trouble as people took advantage of her kindness, but mostly it meant she had a lot of people who loved and cared for her.

GiGi wanted the minutes to move more quickly. She knew watching the clock never helped hurry time. To keep busy she reviewed more stories for the book and checked over some of the characters' names. Finally her grandfather clock chimed 10. It was time to make her big phone call.

"Let the banners wave and the horns blare. I have an announcement to make," GiGi said excitedly, when her friend Sara Bennington answered her phone.

"What has you so excited?" Sara asked.

"The Angels made me do it!" GiGi exclaimed, "I couldn't wait to tell you. I want you to be the first to know." GiGi heard Sara's familiar chuckling on the other end of the phone.

"What the Devil are you going to do about it?" Sara asked. They both chuckled.

"I want to share the book's progress with you. I'm very excited about this new direction," GiGi said.

"Sure seems that way. When will we discuss these changes?"

GiGi answered, "How about my picking up coffee and Danish and meeting at our favorite park bench? The weather is nice. We can people-watch and I'll explain all."

"Sounds good to me," Sara responded and they set a date for 10:30 a.m.

Soon the women were enjoying the sun's warm rays. They sat in the park and watched as boys walked by in their uniform droopy pants or whizzed by on skates and skateboards, diving and jumping in competition with each other. The passing mothers and babies wore identical sports togs. One bright purple outfit out-shined the orange one, and then was out-maneuvered by the flaming red with silver stripes. Mothers jogged along pushing the obligatory baby strollers. For a while, GiGi and Sara sat quietly, gorging on too many sticky Danish, licking their fingers, now and then dropping bits for the inevitable pigeons and robins. The sun felt good as they relaxed. They felt comfortable at their favorite spot in the park and in each other's company.

Finally Sara said, "I know you are dying to tell me your announcement. I must confess I'm curious too – especially the Angel part," she said with her Sara chuckle. "Did you sit on your golden rocking chair high in the clouds surrounded by your Angels – your 'safe place' as you call it?'"

"Of course not," GiGi responded. "That special place is when I need courage to solve a problem. This time was different." She continued, "I thought you'd never ask. How did you manage to wait so long? I was keeping time and you broke your old record." They both laughed.

"Well, let me tell you, it was Roger Angel who did the deciding for me. I had finished three pages of the old book, printed it, and then started off in a different direction, changing much of what I had printed out. I stopped and thought: What am I doing? I began to close the file but then the computer asked if I wanted to save the file. A little box showed a 'yes' highlighted or a 'no'…"

"I bet you hit 'no,'" Sara interjected.

"Uh-uh. What happened was a strong push on my finger for 'yes'. That's how my original draft went into the clouds or wherever all those older versions go. And I don't miss it one bit," said GiGi as she waved her hand in the air as if wiping a slate clean.

"Even after you did all that planning and writing?" Sara asked, recalling the long hours of work her friend had put into her book so far.

"Nope. It feels like it was meant to be. I know that the new draft is going to be a better version of the book and I'm ready to go wherever it takes me. I owe it to my dear Angels – Roger Angel in particular," GiGi said, referring to her long lost love who was always with her in spirit. GiGi had many of these Angels she often called upon. Some were people she knew who had passed on and some were the people still in her life who came to her aid in big and small ways, helping her when she was in need of support or assistance with a problem or task. GiGi depended on them and always trusted in them. "I know my Angels would never steer me wrong," she asserted.

Sara looked at her quizzically and asked, "Roger Angel? You haven't mentioned him in a while. Is he back in the picture?"

"He's never really been out of the picture. I've often wondered how it would have been had I married him rather than Gary. For one thing, sex would not have been a problem. I remember in the car we used to 'neck,' as it was called years ago. Both of us were always aroused and almost went all the way several times. Sometimes I wish we had," GiGi said, adding with a laugh, "I remember my mother telling me years later how my dad would take our dog out for her usual nighttime walk. He would pace the neighborhood searching for Roger's car. If he had discovered us, maybe he would have forced Roger to make an honest woman of me."

Sara and GiGi both chuckled at that.

Then Sara asked, "What about the religious question? How do you think Roger's mother, after what she said, would have reacted? What about your parents?"

GiGi knew Sara was referring to the fact that, even though they really weren't practicing any religion, GiGi's family was culturally Jewish and Roger's family was Presbyterian. In those days that was often an issue when it came to marriage. Interfaith marriages were still rather rare and often families would interfere and break up couples.

GiGi became serious. "I believe we would have formed a 'united front.' We would have said they would have to adjust or they'd lose us."

"It sounds very brave for those days. Do you really think you would have done that?" asked Sara.

GiGi said, "I want to believe it would have been like that. But I must admit that this is now. Looking back I want to put a favorable picture on it. Who knows?"

Sara agreed, "You could be right. But it didn't happen. It's time to let go. I think Roger Angel would agree with me. Now is now. It's time to move on."

GiGi nodded. "You're right. Unfortunately, look where moving on got me then – into a miserable marriage with Gary – and we still had that whole religious problem anyhow because Gary's family was Catholic."

"Yeah. Well I didn't say that moving on was without risk," Sara replied.

GiGi said, "OK. I hear your message and the Angels are tugging at me. I'll let it go and take it in the 'spirits' it was given – ha – 'spirits' I like that."

And so it was.

CHAPTER 2

A SPECIAL FRIENDSHIP, SURROUNDED BY ANGELS

In bed, later on that night, GiGi began to think of her special friendship with Sara Bennington. It must have been at least 30 or more years, she thought. It had endured many traumas and trials while ripening with age and even reached the point where they sometimes could read each other's minds.

"Hers more than mine," GiGi admitted to herself.

It was so comfortable to be in each other's company too. They looked out for each other. GiGi thought, "Sara thinks she's fooling me with those early morning calls. She makes believe it's because she wants to bring me up to date on some news. I know that what she really wants is to make sure I'm OK." With that sweet thought, GiGi thanked her Angels and started to doze off.

But GiGi had a restless night. She kept thinking about the book, the characters. "Oops, need to remember to call them players," she muttered, half asleep. "They're like players in a big life extravaganza. They take turns, urging me to tell their story." That brought the thought about asking Sara how she would feel sharing some of their remembrances in the book. After all, between them they had over 150 years of living.

The friends had helped each other through a lot. They had experienced good, blessedly good, bad and even miserably bad times. Those stories alone could probably take up the whole book. Not that GiGi wanted to do it that way. There were so many exciting things happening now that needed to be written about.

When trauma stories were given to her the people became real. Even though she may never have met them – they became the players who moved about in her mind, sometimes even jostling each other, wanting to be written about. She wondered if all writers and authors had that experience, as if these were real people. Being a writer, if she could call herself one, was certainly interesting and challenging, she reminded herself. She decided to check out these feelings about the characters –no, *the players*- with her next writing class.

How had she wandered from asking Sara about their memories to these thoughts? One thought inevitably leads to another as they make their own way. No point in trying to control them. Then that thought led to thinking about asking Sara to talk a bit about her Nana's psychic abilities. She hadn't talked about that in the five years since Nana died. It could be an interesting future day.

Sara met so many fascinating people now that she was announcing news of the upcoming book! GiGi was even approached in the markets with questions about what was happening. A new thing for her, she usually just shopped. GiGi was always polite with people when being told about their families or being shown the inevitable baby pictures. This was definitely different and sometimes fun too.

Many times these days, Sara would call GiGi with news of some person or another whom she had met at a store or in their building. It was always someone who had a story about some bullying incident in their lives they wanted to share with GiGi for the book. People were coming out of the woodwork, it seemed. Since Sara was talking it up all over town, GiGi was also finding more people stopping her, even strangers, having heard about her book and wanting to tell her their stories. It was a bit overwhelming sometimes to realize how many people had been touched by the issue of bullying. It seemed that it was becoming an epidemic. Having so many people tell her or Sara their stories was certainly giving GiGi a lot to choose from to include in the book and that, indeed, was a good thing. But needing to make choices about what to put in, and what must be left out, often had GiGi worrying and struggling with the book as well.

GiGi thought, "I could either praise Sara or blame her for this latest interest in the book and how it is progressing. Think I'll just let it all happen. My Angels surely will help me figure out what direction to go with the book."

When Sara and GiGi met a couple of days later, the weather had turned cold.

The wind blustered its way; managing to make the women turn in different directions to hold their hats, or else lose them to that great hat catcher in the sky. GiGi pictured Sara's bright blue one and her red tam flying up, up, up into the air like a child's kite that had slipped off its string and rose above the trees and out of reach forever.

"Let's take refuge at my place," GiGi suggested, "It's warm, comfortable and the Angels will keep us company."

Sara agreed and they hurried into the building and up to GiGi's apartment, ending up where one of their favorite little hangings said "Angels Dwell Here." It had been supplied by the local dollar store, their favorite specialty shop.

"I'm always amazed," Sara said looking round the apartment at GiGi's extensive collection of all things Angel-themed. "What fun to see all the new ones you've managed to bring to their proper home."

"It has been fun. Don't forget how many Angels you have gifted me over the years. We all thank you for that. There are the old fashioned ones, the bright cheery ones, and the funny and silly ones. Even the one made of pearls and the latest made of safety pins," GiGi said, listing just a few. "And I love them all."

"But that's not even counting the ones in your bedroom; those that you hang on the venetian blinds. Do you ever worry they'll fall off?" Sara asked, quickly adding, "Oh no, of course not, you never would open those blinds. You might disturb your dear Angels; or they might fly away!"

As usual Sara was right. It always amazed GiGi how a 92-year-old woman and one only 65 could be so similar, especially coming from different backgrounds.

Then, Sara suddenly asked, "Why do you have such a passion for writing your book?"

"Wow, that's a big switch, Sara. What prompted that?" GiGi asked.

"I think it's this special atmosphere. Anything can be talked about now that I'm telling people I'm your 'liaison'," Sara replied.

"Wait a minute. What's this 'liaison' thing?" GiGi asked.

"Well, since I've been talking about your book, when people ask questions I tell them I'm your 'liaison.' Then if they want to tell a story about bullies, they know I'll tell you. Oops. After all these years, I guess I should have remembered to ask you first, huh?" Sara said a bit sheepishly.

Sara looked so sorry that GiGi hastily said, "Not at all. It's all right, of course. It's just sort of getting a little bit ahead of things."

Then, realizing she hadn't answered Sara's question about where the passion for the book started, GiGi added: "Well you know how I hate labels and when people are denigrated with words or deeds for being different. That is bullying or abuse. Its effects can last for years. You know how I can personally attest to that."

Sara nodded, adding "Well, there certainly is a lot of public-ity about bullying of all kinds on TV, radio and the newspapers, plus on 'Twitter' and 'Facebook' too. Even my old school is finally doing something about it."

GiGi said, "I hope people will be encouraged to write letters to the bully even if the letter isn't sent. At least they'll put their feelings down on paper. I know how you and I have done it over the years – and how even not sending it still helped."

Sara knew GiGi was referring to the times over the years that both women had found it helpful to write a letter to someone who had caused them some distress, large or small. Sometimes just the writing of the letter was therapeutic and helpful, even if the letter was never sent. On the other hand, sometimes sending the letter was what helped heal the situation. This was another aspect of what GiGi was advocating in her book.

"So now would it be OK to keep being your 'liaison'?" Sara asked.

Laughing, GiGi told her to keep doing whatever, and said she knew Sara would be discreet. And so it was.

CHAPTER 3

MRS. OLSEN HAS A BULLYING STORY FOR THE BOOK

Several days later, as Sara and GiGi were leaving the food market, someone was calling. "Ms. Bennington, Ms. Bennington, I want to tell you something important." The voice persisted until they could see Mrs. Olsen's chubby little figure in the bright sunlight. She was hurrying and Sara and GiGi were concerned she would trip on the rough pavement.

"Don't rush, Mrs. Olsen, take your time. We'll wait for you." Sara turned to GiGi and said "I wonder what can be so urgent. She usually doesn't walk so fast."

Mrs. Olsen was now abreast of the women, standing next to Sara's bright red Honda Civic. "We're in a bit of a hurry," Sara said, shifting packages into the car. "Our frozen foods will need to get home shortly."

Mrs. Olsen, a little breathless, said "I thought you would want to know about something interesting. Didn't you call yourself a liaison for your friend who is doing a book on bullying? Everyone is talking about it."

Sara glanced at GiGi, questioningly.

GiGi nodded and interjected, "She certainly is and I'm available but this isn't the time or place to talk about it. Can we make an appointment? You can set it up with Sara for a mutually convenient time."

Sara explained they did really need to get home and asked if tomorrow at 3 p.m. in her apartment for tea and the story would be OK.

Mrs. Olsen readily agreed as Sara murmured under her breath, "She's been dying to see my place since I redecorated last year."

When they were seated in the car, GiGi said, "Do we have to wait till people want to see changes to your apartment in order to get their stories? Maybe you should redecorate more often."

Sara grinned as she maneuvered her car out of the parking lot. "I will do whatever sacrifice is necessary, Madame."

Then, turning serious, she said "Mrs. Olsen and her husband are our supers. I wonder if she is having a problem with one of the residents. They are lovely people, work very hard and are stuck between the condo management and the residents. There I go," Sara said sighing, "Guessing again," as she turned into her apartment house's parking lot. "And this garage is another place for bullying – talk about road rage if someone's space is even slightly touched. Maybe that's something she wants to talk about?"

GiGi finally said, "Let it go. We'll know tomorrow, whatever it is."

The next day, Mrs. Olsen rang the bell promptly at 3 p.m., carrying a plate of delicious looking cookies that smelled heavenly. "I never had a chance to bring you my specialties before. They are my home-made Oatmeal and Chocolate Chip Cookies. I hope you enjoy them," she said as she handed the plate to Sara.

"We certainly will enjoy them with our tea," Sara responded, as she lifted the plate up closer to her nose, "they smell fabulous." She suggested Mrs. Olsen and GiGi make themselves comfortable on any of the soft cushioned chairs arranged in a semi-circle facing a large fish tank in her living room.

"I think you may want to share your story first, Mrs. Olsen. Then we can do the tour of my recent redecorating efforts and end up here to relax with tea and your lovely cookies."

Mrs. Olsen nodded. "I'd like that," as she scooted herself back on the chair and nestled herself up against the extra cushions, giving a big relaxed sigh, as she settled in.

As GiGi and Mrs. Olsen sat on Sara's matching comfortable wing chairs in one of GiGi's favorite rooms, they relaxed and waited for Sara to make tea. Almost on cue, the brightly colored, exotic looking fish danced in and out of all the special plants and caves Sara had provided for their and her enjoyment.

It was a challenge as GiGi tried to remember their names, like Sammy and Peter and Angela and Susie – but Sara knew them all, even their scientific names – and she often told GiGi which ones were doing whatever tropical fish like to do.

After a few minutes, Sara came back into the room, named a few more fish as she pointed out which was which. Finally she sat down and asked Mrs. Olsen if she wanted to begin her story.

Mrs. Olsen started. "As you may know, Ms. Bennington, I travel to the city every week to visit my cousin. Last time we went to a special program. The actors were doing a show about bullying. I was definitely interested 'cause I knew about the book. Well, plus some of what happens out here too." Mrs. Olsen said, "The auditorium was darkish and gloomy. Nothing was on the stage except for lots of blank boards fastened to poles. Then some lights flickered on and off. Then the stage lit up with eight actors standing near the boards. Then a loud voice suddenly said: 'Finally, a light is exposing our stories and we need your help. We invite a few members of the audience to form a line against the wall.' Right away some people jumped up and formed the line. Then the voice said 'We invite you to come forward to pick up a board. Then turn it around so the audience can read it.' One of the actors started by picking up a board, he turned it around so the audience could shout out 'Bullying in the home.' Then another marched to the other side of the auditorium. Then more boards were picked up and turned so that the audience could now shout out 'Bullying in the school', 'Bullying on the computer.' Soon there were about 22 different ones. There were ethnic, religious, sexual and lots more. I don't think most people knew how many different kinds of bullying there were. Those signs made quite a display as bright lights shined on each one of them, one at a time."

Sara and GiGi looked at each other and both said, almost in chorus, "I had no idea!"

Mrs. Olsen nodded and continued her story. "Finally, a voice thanked everyone. The actors asked the audience which stories they wanted to hear. There were many votes for the Internet and school, and just as many for sexual and ethnic identity."

Mrs. Olsen continued, "Then the stage went dark except for a spotlight shining on a large box on the stage. It had 'Costumes' painted on the side. It was filled with different hats and large and small scarves. There were lots of colors and sizes. Then the actors picked out their costumes. The lights went down again and then came up on a kitchen scene. There was the father yelling at his son. The father told Billy how he was no good and slapped him across the face. And then he told him how he had made him kick the cat out the door for messing up the kitchen because stupid 15-year-old Billy forgot to take out the garbage again. He told Billy to get out and get down to the school bus. The boy was upset as he kicked his way down the driveway. Then he snatched a boy's cap and called him a fag. He was still angry and pushed and pulled the younger children waiting for the bus. After a while the lights went down again.

"Next was a family in bright clothes sitting at a picnic table in the park. They were talking in a foreign language. Then Billy and his friends came, riding skateboards. They were dressed in baggy pants and torn shirts and those backwards baseball caps. They were fooling around. Billy was still angry and kept looking at the family. He said nasty things to them like some people should stay home in their own country. Then he kept skating around the table. Suddenly, he pulled a scarf off one of the younger girls and held it up like a victory flag. Then his friends joined in the skating and making threatening motions. Suddenly, one of the boys shouted to look out as the park police were coming. They left quickly.

"Afterwards, they acted out a few more scenes about other kinds of bullying," Mrs. Olsen explained. "It certainly was an education."

Mrs. Olsen continued, "Then the actors started to tell why they felt bullied, or when they had done the bullying. In the middle of this, a young woman rushed to the stage in tears. She cried out that she had that happen when she first came here. We all thought she was one of the actors. We were surprised when the actors said she was from the audience. It wasn't unusual. Then one of the actors took her backstage to make her feel better. I guess they probably gave her information on where to get help. Then the actors finished telling their reasons for being a bully or a victim. Then they ended handing out information on where and how to get help like First Call for Help, United Way, churches, schools, synagogues. I noticed people even asking for more than one copy. You could hear the people talking about how true to life it was. I felt very lucky to see it," Mrs. Olsen said.

GiGi and Sara listened intently to what Mrs. Olsen was saying and when she finished, the two women each took a deep breath, digesting all the details. Sara spoke first saying "Wow that sounds like an intense performance. I can tell from what you shared that you were very moved by the experience."

GiGi was very interested in the performance and asked, "Do you know if this was a one-time performance or do they do this often? I'd love to see this myself. It certainly is exactly what my book is all about."

Mrs. Olsen said she wasn't sure about how often the performance was being presented or where else it might be held.

GiGi asked Mrs. Olsen some information about the acting group and where she might find them.

Mrs. Olsen said she would get the printed material and pass it along.

They talked excitedly about the show for some time and then Sara noticed Mrs. Olsen start to look around the room checking out some of the decorations that were new.

Sara rose and suggested it might be time for them to take the tour. Mrs. Olsen was delighted and practically jumped up from her seat to begin. Throughout the short tour the visitor kept commenting on how "Everything fits so nicely together."

They then returned to the family room where Sara had served tea and the melt-in-your-mouth cookies Mrs. Olsen had brought.

They both thanked her for taking the time to tell them her story. It could be very helpful. There was more chatting and around 4 O'clock, Mrs. Olsen said she had to leave.

Sara and GiGi were left with their impressions of the afternoon. GiGi was excited about the acting group and Sara was concerned about the stories that were *not* told.

GiGi asked Sara what she meant by "not told." Sara said she felt that Mrs. Olsen could have told many bullying stories about the residents in this building — but worries about her job prevented any of those accounts, even with discreet people like herself and GiGi.

GiGi agreed noting "There are plenty of stories about bullying that will never be told; sadly, on account of too much fear of reprisal. Maybe that booklet the acting group had handed out could have some good information. Who knows, maybe it would be good to include a listing in the back of the book for resources people could use."

"Good idea," Sara agreed, adding "But you know it's always my hope that someday all the stories will be told."

"That's my Sara, ever so hopeful," GiGi replied with a smile. Then she got up from her chair and said "Well, I must be going if I want to catch my program while I nibble on my dinner."

"Would you like to take along some cookies?" Sara asked.

"I wouldn't dream of taking any away. And now, away I go," GiGi said with a smile. They hugged and GiGi went on her way, leaving Sara with the remaining cookies and her interesting fish.

CHAPTER 4

SARA'S COUSIN SHIRLEY DIED

The following morning Sara called before 9 a.m., which was very unusual. Both women liked to wake slowly and to start the day relaxed, enjoying breakfast. There was no work place to rush to. They could be relaxed. Though sometimes GiGi thought they were busier than ever.

When Sara called that early, GiGi realized she was upset. It sounded like she had been crying.

"Sara, what's wrong. What's happened?" and before she could say more, Sara blurted out, "My cousin Shirley died. You remember her?"

"Of course I do, she was just a year and a half younger than you. You haven't seen her in a long time..."

"But that's it. We haven't seen each other for years, ever since my parents' 75th anniversary party 15 years ago."

GiGi said, "I know you're upset. But what does their anniversary have to do with her dying?"

"It's because I invited her to their party — and then uninvited her," Sara confessed.

"That doesn't sound like you, Sara," GiGi said, "Why would you do that?"

"I don't know. It's just too much for now. Sorry I called. I just want to be alone and quiet for a while. I'll get back to you later when I feel better. Promise," Sara said.

Over the years, GiGi had learned that when Sara said "promise" she just needed some alone time. She needed to think things over. Then she would be back to talk. Since she and GiGi reacted similarly, they'd learned to respect each other. GiGi could relax and wait for

Sara's call or visit, whatever she decided was best.

After lunch, Sara called and said she'd be right over. When she got there all she said was, "Your Angels made me do it!"

GiGi realized that "leaving things to whatever was best" often really meant waiting for her Angels to take over and, once again, so it was.

"How did my Angels get into this?" GiGi asked, knowing it was not unusual for them to appear at the most opportune places.

"They certainly helped you with your letters," Sara reminded her. "Anyhow they said I should send my cousin a letter."

GiGi told Sara she agreed.

Thinking back on her 92 years, the therapy sessions and all the friends that filled her life and the many difficulties overcome, GiGi said, "Sure there were many traumas that were dealt with and then I was able to enjoy the good times – the productive times – that were part of my life as well. The letters, helped along the way. Of course, there are some I'd write differently today."

GiGi recalled one of her unsent letters to her ex, "As I look back, it definitely would be written differently today. I have that safe place now where no one can ever harm me. It's my special gold rocking chair, high in the clouds, surrounded by all my Angels – forming a chain that is invincible."

Suddenly GiGi asked, "Would you like to hear my unsent letter to Gary from eons ago?"

Sara nodded and GiGi took out a yellowed page from at least 50 years ago. As usual, GiGi saved every piece of paper – important or not – and this one was definitely important to her, even though it just said "Gary, We need to talk about money..." and there it ended, waiting for another day. Written on that same yellow sheet was a real letter – not sent but written many years later when the time must have been just right.

Gary,

This is about when you were the manager of the Atlanta branch and made frequent trips to the New York office. Many times one of the salesmen would accompany you and since most of the office families had one car, it was necessary for some wife to drive you all to the airport. It was usually me. I didn't mind except for the times when you were the only one going. Then it would be a silent battle over when you would dole out the money needed for when you were absent.

I remember too well, the noise, hustle and bustle, infants crying, teenagers roaming the vast area of the airport, checking out something to keep them busy, parents frustrated at frequent delays and the times standing on the ticket line next to you, and then on the line just before boarding, waiting for the money. Feeling humiliated, embarrassed as maybe someone would overhear us and the final "well, here"— unable to make a fuss — just like the frequent times you were drunk. After all, if that happened you might lose your job and where would we be? So I was the "good" little wife, with no mind of her own, no opinion of her own, all to keep the peace.

But one day this will change, I would pledge to myself – dramatically change – and I will be in a position to support and protect the family minus you.

Your ex-wife

Sara nodded her head. "I remember you telling me about it, then. What a difference. You must be very proud of how you've changed and all the traumas you've overcome."

Then GiGi and Sara both laughed and agreed that it took a heck of a lot of hard work for GiGi to be truly herself now.

"I know how much the letters helped," Sara continued, as the two old friends both smiled.

The two sat quietly, sipping coffee, relaxed, comfortable in the day, each other's company and special memories.

Then in a mock firm voice, GiGi said "But you better get your own Angels the next time. Who was it who said 'if you don't use them, you'll lose them'?"

"You are right,' Sara smiled. "I guess yours just seemed more convenient. Anyhow, aren't they all part of a family. Or did we agree they had teams? So you had your team and I had mine."

The friends both chuckled at the idea again. They had agreed that several Angel teams could become a family. The Angels had helped GiGi when she had that bad fall – as well as all the other times when they had helped both of them.

Now it was time for Sara to head home and start the letter – or she knew she'd soon be getting tugged by her Angels and GiGi. So off she went.

Several times during the next few days GiGi thought again about Sara and their friendship, how much it meant to her. In the telling, and sometimes retelling, of past traumas, her reaction was always the same. Sara listened, seldom interrupting. On the other hand, sometimes when a friend was describing an incident, GiGi thought," I've interrupted with a similar story. Soon the conversation becomes my story. It has happened to me too many times as well. Usually the original storyteller becomes silent and probably thinks 'Well, at least I tried.'"

But Sara's reaction was different. She really listened – without interruptions – unless she was asked for her thoughts, of course.

Then GiGi thought about the book. It was going to be about "when a person has no respect for another person."

She wondered how did interrupting another person mean abuse or bullying? Those words seemed too strong. Maybe thoughtless or inconsiderate would be better. They still meant not respecting the other person. Maybe the way it could be handled was for the storyteller to say in a respectful way, "Excuse me. May I finish my story? It's important to me."

GiGi thought, "I'll discuss it with Sara. Bet she says 'Leave it to our Angels. They'll find good words to say.'"

Thinking back, GiGi remembered Sara's reaction when she told her how she appreciated their friendship – actually treasured it. Sara had blushed slightly and turned towards GiGi and said "It goes both ways, and may it ever be so."

"True," GiGi remembered saying cheerily, "At least we have to the end of time. Or put another way – till the book gets published."

"Well, that was one way of putting it," Sara had responded, "You certainly have a knack of getting the book mentioned whenever. And now it's my turn to mention lunch. I'm famished. How about food for a change? You were always interested in that subject before."

GiGi remembered answering "Have to keep my spirits up in order to do the book and, ha, ha – that's my final word."

The two had laughed and started walking to their favorite Italian restaurant. "It's my treat this time – another final word," GiGi had said firmly.

Sara had smiled and then she said, "May I say 'OK' for my final word?"

As they approached the restaurant this afternoon, it was obviously busier than usual. It looked like they were giving away the food – an "it's on us" come-on.

When they entered, their favorite waitress waved towards a table that was being cleared. They moved quickly. The table was at the window they preferred. It didn't take long to be cleaned. The usual candle and small vase with a rose appeared. Their silverware, napkins and hot garlic bread were next. It was time to pick something yummy from the menus handed to them.

Sara was quick at making her choice. GiGi always took extra time. There were so many yummy choices. Finally, she made the big decision and they could relax.

While waiting for lunch, GiGi told Sara she was thinking of writing another book—when this one was finished, of course.

"Is it going to be about Devils this time?" Sara asked with a big grin, "They need attention too, you know."

"You are so wrong. This time it will be about friendships — maybe one like ours. What do you think of that idea?"

Sara looked very solemn and said "I think that's a wonderful theme. We have such a good one. Sometimes when I try to figure out how it happened the only answer is it just did. From the moment you greeted me at the Unitarian Fellowship door, as a 35-year-old pregnant mom with 2-year-old Sybil clinging to my legs. Your warm welcome made me feel so comfortable. Then you led us inside to be greeted by your friends. And Sybil, who usually was shy with strangers, just laughed and giggled at the attention. I knew this definitely was our home."

They smiled at each other – happy with their friendship memories.

As GiGi relaxed waiting for their choices, she thought about Sybil and how happy she was when Sheila was born. How much alike they seemed in so many ways—resembling Sara, or at least Sheila did more than Sybil. Sybil had much of her father, Jon, in her too. Maybe Sheila had some of her own father in her but since he died before she was born, GiGi never had the chance to meet him. Sometimes when the girls were older and playing together their strong resemblance to Sara was even more evident.

Before long their meals were served. It was time to enjoy the house salad and garlic bread. GiGi's favorite was eggplant parmigiana with angel hair – what else?

Sara always liked chicken cacciatore.

Then came the usual sharing of their meals.

After dividing the check evenly, they nodded approval to their waitress and simultaneously pronounced "It's coffee ice cream time." And so it was.

CHAPTER 5

SARA HEADS TO VERMONT FOR A REUNION AND MEETS CHRISSIE

Sara called after 10 the next morning. She had important news – she was going to visit some old college chums in Vermont. On the return trip home she would attend Shirley's Memorial service.

GiGi asked "Have you finished her letter yet?"

Sara's response was "I want to think about the approach. Maybe read it to the family."

This seemed rather dramatic to GiGi but she said nothing. She hoped Sara and her Angels would eventually figure it out.

"Since I'm not leaving till tomorrow, want to come over and help me pick out my wardrobe?" Sara asked.

GiGi thought: Sara, the fashion guru, asking me to help pick out her clothes. GiGi primly said, "I'd be pleased to help," and almost smirked. Then she realized Sara was serious. That meant she was really upset about her cousin's death and facing her family. She needed company. GiGi wondered if she had thought about asking her daughters to accompany her. She realized it would have been dismissed. They probably wouldn't have remembered Shirley and her family.

When GiGi entered the apartment Sara asked if GiGi wanted iced tea. "I'll bring it into the bedroom. Meet you there."

GiGi liked Sara's bedroom with its huge white sleigh bed that was always covered with brightly colored pillows. Her oversized armoire nicely balanced the rest of the room with its celadon green carpet and white decorated dressers. There were flowers and green leaves in pretty colored vases sitting on the floor or clustered on small tables. Her favorite was the comfortable flowered chaise lounge for relaxing. Though green wasn't her favorite color – at least on herself. It seemed just right here.

GiGi made herself comfortable on the chaise lounge. Then waited for the display of possible outfits Sara would bring out for her approval.

Before Sara could bring in the tea, her younger daughter Sheila came into the room very upset. She had seen something that disturbed her.

"It's here again," Sheila said in an anguished tone.

When she saw GiGi, she ran out of the room. Sara and GiGi shared a knowing look and Sara went off to console her daughter.

GiGi realized it must have been the "lint in the mirror thing" again. Though normally she would have left, she decided to stay and offer whatever comfort would be needed.

Sara returned shortly and said that Sheila was going out with friends. That seemed the best thing for her at the moment. GiGi offered to leave. But Sara asked her to stay and just continue normally. She wanted GiGi to help pick out clothes. GiGi realized she needed company even more than before and stayed.

Sara asked GiGi again about tea. They agreed hot tea this time. Sara left to make it. She returned shortly afterward with their favorite tea – peppermint. It was just right. No need to say anything.

GiGi knew the story of the "mirror thing." Its mysterious meaning concerned her as much as it did Sara.

Sara and GiGi quietly sipped their tea and each tried to push thoughts of the mirror and the lint out of their heads for now.

After they had relaxed for a while, Sara decided she needed to start deciding on her wardrobe. As she was picking out some dresses she said "I was just reminded about my niece Molly's wedding announcement. I wonder if you would be willing to accompany me as my so-called date."

GiGi immediately exclaimed "Oh Sara, you know how I hate those occasions. Please pick someone else. You know how loud music drives me crazy. I could go on and on."

"There's no need to be so dramatic," Sara said, "But it would mean a lot to me if you came," then Sara said no more.

GiGi knew she was working some guilt on her. She also knew, as well as Sara did, that it would, of course, work in the long run. They had helped each other out so many times. How could she refuse?

GiGi, mused half out loud, "That's what friends are for, isn't it?"

Sara smiled and said, also half out loud, "Think of what I'll owe you!"

After much discussion it was decided GiGi needed a dress for the occasion. They made plans to shop for it when Sara returned from Vermont and Shirley's memorial service.

Sara said "Now it's time to bring out my possibles." She brought out three outfits for her visit. GiGi loved them all, especially the black sheath dress with the gold jewelry, purse and shoes to complete it. She also loved the red tunic and pants.

She guessed Sara planned on lots of partying in Vermont. Her soft blue pants suit and flowery silk scarf seemed just right for the memorial service. GiGi gave her approval to all.

It was time to go out again. They admitted some fresh air was needed.

GiGi suggested, "How about a short stop at our favorite deli and then visit our park bench. It's still a lovely day and after lunch there may still be people for watching." They were soon on their way.

It was indeed a lovely day. Since it was a school day, there were fewer people to watch. Instead the pigeons had the friends' attention. Squabbling, pushing and poking, the birds made as much noise as possible in their ferocious fights over the doughnut crumbs they dropped.

Sara and GiGi took turns betting which ones would be victorious. It always seemed to be the most aggressive – what a surprise – there were bullies among the birds as well.

Maybe the pigeons' bullying antics prompted Sara's next question. She asked GiGi what was new with the book. GiGi told her about the meanings of abuse and bullying vs. being inconsiderate or thoughtless.

"I'd like to talk about that when I get back," Sara said. "This time we have our Angel teams to help us. But you have to promise not to talk to them about it before I get back."

Laughing, GiGi agreed.

They chatted, watching the few people passing. The pigeons were now looking elsewhere for crumbs. It was still sunny and warm and they relaxed, not speaking, just enjoying the day and each other's company.

GiGi thought, there aren't many people who can sit, not speak and still enjoy each other's company when Sara said, "I know what you're thinking. It's definitely true. We are two very lucky people to know and care for each other for all these years."

When Sara returned from her Vermont trip she was all excited. Her visit with her friends had been a lot of fun. When she shared her letter dilemma they gave her good ideas.

"Did you meet anyone in particular," GiGi asked, "You were all set with those stunning clothes."

"As a matter of fact, I did meet a couple of interesting men – especially one. He lives two states away," Sara said.

"Maybe he'll 'just have' some relatives or business here. You could be surprised," GiGi said. "Two states isn't that far. Get your Angels to help."

"Yeah – I did sort of like him. We had a lot in common. We'll see."

GiGi sat thinking about how Sara was usually the center of attention, whether with men or women. She had that personality that drew you to her. She was always interested in others and seemingly not aware of her effect on them.

"And what interesting people did you meet on the train?" GiGi asked. She knew that Sara must have made friends with half the passengers. GiGi was sure she read them her Tarot cards as well.

Sara's readings were a bit different from most people's, GiGi recalled. She used the round "Mother Peace" cards that were beautifully illustrated and easily interpreted. Sara would lay out the cards in a special pattern. Since they were round, she would ask the other person to interpret the upright, reverse or tilted position the cards were in – whatever position was comfortable. It always amazed GiGi and the other person how often the readings were so accurate. GiGi thought having the other person determine the card's position made them feel comfortable. Even when the cards showed something they didn't want to hear. Maybe they had their own Angels to help position the cards.

Sara said "I met Chrissie, a pretty redhead with sparkly blue eyes. She was dressed in an attractive blue outfit to complement her eyes. She was on her long distance way to Florida."

"Was there a particular reason for this long distance trip?" GiGi asked.

GiGi knew she would get some details today. Follow up details would come later as well. Sara had that look she often got when she was picking up a new stray. "She will definitely keep in touch with this young woman," GiGi thought as she waited for Sara to answer her question.

"It seems Chrissie was diagnosed with breast cancer and had sent her parents a letter to ask if she could return home. When she left 15 years before, mean and nasty words were exchanged. It took a lot of courage for her to write them," Sara explained.

Sara's eyes and GiGi's teared up as Sara told of Chrissie's trip and her parents' letter eagerly welcoming her back.

As GiGi listened she was also remembering all the letters that were written and sent, written but not sent and too many times unwritten. She looked at Sara and they both nodded, understanding each other's feelings. There were tears because Chrissie was able to write to her parents and because of their kind welcoming letter back to her. The past could be forgotten for now. They would be able to re-establish a relationship and love would help to heal. "Bless Chrissie for taking that big step of writing and her parents for writing back," GiGi thought.

GiGi asked Sara if she had done a reading for Chrissie. GiGi was assured it was a big part of their time together.

Sara said Chrissie liked the reading and felt it was a big help in alleviating some misgivings she was feeling. Sara said she hoped Chrissie would call on her Angels – she certainly needed them. GiGi said she hoped so too.

Changing the subject, GiGi asked, "Did you finish the Shirley letter. How did it work out?"

"I decided not to share it with the whole family only with her husband, Tim," Sara said.

"Thank goodness," GiGi thought. "The Angels probably tugged at her and possibly helped to avoid a scene with a lot of people. One person would have been enough."

"He was very understanding," Sara said. "He was sure Shirley would have forgiven me."

GiGi thought about Sara's previous distress. This was important. GiGi hoped that now her friend would be able to forgive herself.

Sara said "I want to tell you about the letter and then some of my second thoughts about all this."

"Second thoughts – what kind of second thoughts are you having?" GiGi asked.

"Well, let me share the letter first," Sara said and she began:

Dear Shirley,

After hearing from your son Robert, I agree with him that my be-havior was hurtful. It was never intended to do that and for that I am very sorry.

When I invited you to my parent's 75th anniversary party, I was not aware of the problems you and Herb were having. He made it very clear that he would not attend if you were coming.

Since he was my only source of help for my parents, I depended on him to do many things I could not since I was working full time as well as being three hours away from them.

Since I couldn't take the chance that he would stop helping, and they were needy at the time, I felt it necessary to un-invite you to the party.

In retrospect, I now realize that it was the wrong thing to do — I should have invited both of you, no matter your relationship.

I am truly sorry for my action and hope you will find it in your heart to forgive me.

With Love,

Sara

"Have you forgiven yourself? GiGi asked "My Angels tell me you have not totally forgiven yourself. Are they on to something?"

Sara blushed and said, "Those Angels certainly were right. I haven't settled it in my mind yet."

Then she proceeded to tell GiGi that she and her family were never close to Shirley and her family. She hadn't been invited to any of Shirley's anniversary parties for her parents. Then Sara added she was sincere with the letter she gave Tim. Later she found out that Shirley and her brother Herb had forgiven each other. They had been on good terms for the last seven or eight years.

"Yes, I know Tim said Shirley would have forgiven me," Sara said. "But on my return train trip, I thought, I wonder why Shirley hadn't written to me about how she felt. After all she was a therapist. Oh well, guess they're only human too."

There it was – the finally written, unsent letter from Sara to Shirley and the never written letter from Shirley to Sara.

Trying to make sense of all this, GiGi said, "I don't think that has anything to do with it. In any case, if the people from opposite sides of this invitation had sent letters to each other explaining their feelings it might have been different."

Sara said, with great emphasis, "Never, ever will I fail to invite people no matter how they feel about other guests. Talk about sent and unsent, even unwritten letters. I wish I had known something about this years ago. Maybe I would have done the right thing. Let them handle their problems themselves; and why didn't my Angels help me?"

GiGi reminded her that she had not called them for help for a long time. Sara giggled and said "They certainly are my team now."

GiGi began to see the real Sara again. She thought they certainly had enough of that stuff. The book would wait for someone else to write about invitations. There were always too many to write anyway, with birthdays, graduations, weddings. One could name dozens in a person's life and the possible mix-ups.

Then GiGi suggested they should go for some yummy coffee ice cream. Sara liked the idea – just to celebrate that all was well again, of course.

And so it was.

CHAPTER 6

SARA IS WORRIED ABOUT CHRISSIE

"I was beginning to worry," was Sara's greeting a few days later. At that, GiGi began to worry about what worried her. "Come on Angels – help her," GiGi thought, maybe the Shirley thing was still upsetting her.

"I finally heard from Chrissie. She's OK, I'm not worried now," Sara continued.

"Thanks Angels," GiGi uttered softly and waited for the latest.

"You remember Chrissie that pretty redhead on her way to Florida?" she asked.

GiGi responded "How could I forget your description of her and the blue outfit."

"Well, before she left Florida she had told her parents about being sexually abused by her older brother and uncle. They didn't believe her. That's when they exchanged angry words and she left home."

GiGi didn't say a word. Sara was so upset over anyone having to go through all of that as a young teenager. It was bad enough for anyone – but to have her parents not believe her and not try to help. It was just too much.

"Sara, is Chrissie all right now?

"Well, I never told you the whole train trip story – the Tarot influence, how my Angels suggested a talk with Chrissie about making her own safe place, to remind her that she had Angels to help whenever she needed them."

"Now you tell me," said GiGi. "So when did Chrissie tell you her latest news?"

"She called last night and said that now her parents believed her," Sara said, adding, "Her brother and uncle were found with teenagers and the girls were bringing charges."

"How sad that it had to take these circumstances to help her parents understand. In any case, at least it happened," GiGi thought.

Then GiGi and Sara talked about how hard it must be for Chrissie's parents. Her brother had helped them when the father lost his job.

Sara softly said, "Imagine finding out that your child did those awful things?"

Then Sara told GiGi that Chrissie had forgiven her parents for not believing her. She wasn't sure she could have done the same.

"I think my Angels would have had to do some heavy tugging," Sara said softly.

GiGi didn't have any answer. She thanked Sara for sharing Chrissie's story especially that Chrissie said it was OK to put it in the book.

"By the way," said Sara "I meant to ask if you spell Angel with a capital 'A' or use the lower case 'a' in the book."

"What made you think of that?" GiGi asked.

"Chrissie just wondered how you did it," Sara said.

"I never even thought about it before," said GiGi. "It's just automatic to use capitals for them. I like it. Sort of elevates them even higher – if that's possible."

The women laughed and ended their conversation on that note.

The next day it was time for a more serious conversation.

"My Mother – that's the letter I need to write," exclaimed Sara on her early morning wake-up call the next day. It wasn't really a wake-up call since it was 10:15 a.m. It was Sara's customary type of statement. GiGi waited.

"I've been thinking of Chrissie's forgiveness of her parents. Maybe it's time for me to do that with my mom, at least in a letter to her.

What do you think?" Sara inquired.

"Sounds good to me," GiGi answered.

"I'm not sure how good it will be – I've been tugged at by my Angels," Sara said. "Guess I'm ready now."

GiGi smiled but said nothing. She thought about how Sara had avoided talking about her unsent letter to her mother.

"You know how long it's been since I was willing to even think about it," Sara said. "Then Chrissie's call reminded me how helpful those letters are. She told me that she had written 'unsent' letters to her brother and uncle. She felt that this is what made it possible to forgive her parents."

GiGi mentally applauded Chrissie and her Angels and waited.

"So I guess it is time. I'll do it today and show it to you afterward," Sara said confidently.

"There's no need for that, Sara," GiGi responded.

"Yes, there is. You're my best friend. I want to share it with you," Sara declared.

"Do you remember about your mom when you changed your name?" GiGi asked. "Who would have imagined dropping the 'h' would make such a difference to her?"

"Remember how angry she was and the nasty things she said? Even saying 'now you'll be just like that slut in the movies,'" Sara said. "We never found out who she meant. Then you reminded me that 'Sara' was still 'Sarah' and that my mom was still the same mom. At times difficult she was, but the same despite the Alzheimer's that was taking over. You were such a help. I want to share this one too."

"Well, whatever you wish," GiGi said. "Good luck and now good-bye or I'll be tempted to tug at you myself."

Her familiar Sara chuckle came over the wire, "Thanks to you. Goodbye."

The two friends hung up.

Then, not smiling, GiGi thought again of how Sara's mom had two distinct ways of picturing her – "Sarah" and the "Sara" who changed the spelling of her given name to "Sara." Somehow the dropping of that letter disturbed her mother deeply. There must have been more to it than just a dropped letter because the mother likened her own daughter to some "slut," from the movies. How could she have been so cruel to Sara over such a thing as the spelling of her own name? Why do people hurt other people so – especially people who love each other?

GiGi was lost in this thought for quite some time. Maybe she was always caught in this thought in some way or another because it was making its way into the book over and over with different names and stories but, underlying it all, it was always there.

CHAPTER 7

SARA SHARES A LETTER TO HER MOM AND GIGI TELLS ANA'S STORY

GiGi and Sara were busy during the following few days. Sara had her meetings. GiGi had the writers' group.

Sara called a week later. "What do you want to do first, my 'Mother letter' or Chinese food?"

"You certainly don't give me much choice, GiGi complained, "That letter or my favorite food."

"Who said it would be easy," Sara chuckled, "choosing can be difficult so I'll let you decide, this time anyway."

They made plans to meet at the new Thai restaurant at 12:30 p.m.

When Sara arrived and joined GiGi at the table, she grinned.

"I take it back. Let's enjoy lunch – then we can have the rest of the afternoon for the letter," Sara said.

GiGi readily agreed. Then they had to make the usual difficult choices. The menu was always so tempting – so "come on choose me." No matter which the women chose, at least they would be sharing. There were always at least two goodies to pick. They never could understand people who didn't share. Then they decided it must be a dietary problem and not selfishness. They certainly didn't have that problem. They enjoyed sharing with a small or large group. Many times they enjoyed a dish never tried before.

"What do you think of 'Thai Lo Mein' and 'Sweet and Sour Chicken'?" asked Sara. "We can compare to similar selections at our favorite Chinese restaurant next time. That is if it hasn't changed to half Thai and Japanese on our next visit."

The food arrived shortly and it looked delicious, as usual. The longtime friends each enjoyed their choices, then decided to skip dessert and go back to GiGi's place to relax and go over Sara's letter.

Finally they were sitting on the sofa, with a big box of tissues GiGi had placed between them, and Sara began:

Mother,

It's not easy but it's time to tell you how hard it was living a lie — our supposedly happy home and the reality. I suspect you probably felt the same.

I know it must have been difficult raising three different children with that fourth so-called "child." He was always drunk and not available to help. Yes, he did work every day. He did bring you his pay check. That was his fathering. Maybe his dad did the same — his father model.

I want to thank you for all the basics you gave us to help us become responsible adults, though it took some of us a lot longer to reach that goal.

I want to thank you for pushing us all to learn sign language. This helped brother Johnny in his challenged life — coping with being deaf in a hearing world. If you hadn't done that, his life might have been harder.

I want to thank you for helping us graduate high school, especially when we didn't want to stay in school.

I want to thank you for encouraging sister Kate to go into the service way back then.

That attitude was frowned on for girls. They should only get married and have babies.

I want to thank you for finally understanding the breakup of my marriage to Jonathan. Your support was a big help.

I want to thank you for many other things. But these are enough for

*now. I hope that wherever you are — you can be proud of the many good
things you did in raising us.*

I love you, Mom.

Sara

The two women took their tissues and for a long time nothing was
said. Nothing needed to be. It had all been said in Sara's letter. After a
while they hugged goodbye and Sara headed home.

GiGi called Sara a few days later. She was concerned because their
friend Ana told her about Ana's daughter, Lori. It happened while Lori
was working as a home health care aide and had made Lori very upset.

"When did Lori start to work?" asked Sara. "She is such a lovely
young woman. No matter what work she does, I know how conscien-
tious she is — a real earthly Angel. People are lucky to have her."

"I know," GiGi agreed. "That's why it's so upsetting to her."

Then GiGi repeated what Ana told her about Lori. "It seems an
elderly gentleman for whom Lori had been caring for almost a-year-
and-a-half had to go to a nursing home. His family had to go on an
extended business trip. On their return they requested she'd continue
to work for them. To her horror he had developed serious bed sores. In
all the time Lori had cared for him he never had a single sore. She and
his family had to turn him every two hours to prevent any new sores
and not inflame the old ones. Lori said that his family was furious with
the unacceptable inattention he had at the nursing home. They sent the
home a letter accusing them of all kinds of abuse in allowing this to oc-
cur. Luckily, the family took this seriously. They plan to take additional
action so it won't happen to anyone else."

As she was recounting the story GiGi felt a tug. Her Angels had a
message. "There were many good nursing homes. Don't condemn all."

When GiGi mentioned this to Sara, Sara agreed, "My Nana had

wonderful care at her nursing home. They couldn't have been better. She loved them and they loved her." Sara added her Angels had tugged at her too.

GiGi remarked, "The 'teams' were certainly keeping us in line. Never condemn everyone because of a few bad apples."

Ana's story was on GiGi's mind as she and Sara sat people-watching a few days later. It was a warm, sunny day. The clouds were sort of ambling along – their different shapes moving and changing as GiGi watched. She was fascinated by the various forms they took. Then just as suddenly they would change into another one. Maybe a horse or mule would become a dragon huffing and puffing. There were always surprises to be viewed.

"You seem preoccupied. What is so fascinating today?" Sara inquired but got no response at first as GiGi was totally in the clouds, it seemed.

This had happened so many times before; the women would study the clouds and guess what the forms were. Then the clouds would change into something else. They were always changing, sometimes right over them or as they slowly drifted on. It always made the two friends feel like little kids again so much to be sitting in the soft green grass, not uncomfortable park benches. But GiGi certainly knew if she tried the green grass – well she might not get up again. Whatever, the cloud spectacles never failed to give pleasure.

"But there is something on your mind today," Sara continued probing her preoccupied friend, "it's not just the clouds, right?"

"I've been thinking about Ana and her Angels," GiGi explained, "How they must have worked to protect her when she was coming to America."

"I know. She's been here almost forever it seems," Sara said. "She's like us – an American citizen."

"That's true, Sara, but she traveled here in her mother's womb and now Ana told me she has been worrying about that trip and its implications," GiGi stated. "She told me all about it. Her mother had told her it was a very tough boat trip. Everyone huddled together like cattle. They were frightened and worried they might not reach America. They might have to return to their home country in South America. They might drown in the rough seas and no one would find them. Luckily they arrived safely and Ana was born three months later in New York City, 45 years ago."

"But her mother's dead. Why is Ana so worried now? How does that affect her now?" Sara asked.

"Because there are some people who believe if your parents were not citizens, you are not entitled to be a citizen," GiGi replied.

"But that doesn't make sense. The Constitution says that you're a citizen automatically if you're born here. It's the law. That should settle it," Sara declared.

"I hope so, Sara. But there are some people who want to change the law. That's what Ana is worried about. She has friends and relatives who could be affected. I gave her the name of an attorney who handles these problems," GiGi said, adding, "Hope it helps."

"Me too," Sara said with a little worry now creeping into her mind as well.

Then as if they both needed a distraction from this new worry for their friend Ana, the women decided to do more cloud watching. Soon they had a lively discussion about one that looked like a puppy dog to GiGi. Sara was equally convinced it was a cottage. GiGi's puppy's tail was smoke coming from a chimney. Of course neither was right or wrong. Then it changed dramatically as it drifted on. So much for vivid imaginations and clouds on a sunny day. The clouds were playing their tricks on the two friends – and having their own fun too.

CHAPTER 8

SHEILA SEES SOMETHING

S everal days later, Sara and GiGi found themselves in the park again.
"By the way," Sara remarked as she and GiGi walked along one
of the park's many winding paths. "We usually try to avoid the constant
skaters, hikers and strollers. I think they're doing most of the dodg-
ing today – to avoid you and that walker. It's a bit of a switch, isn't it?
They're avoiding us."

"And just think – now I carry my own walking seat. There's no
need to always call after you 'save a seat for me.' Though you'll probably have to do that again once I've worked my way back to using only
the cane," GiGi said, confident that it would happen.

"It would be my pleasure to see you doing that again and calling
out to me: 'Save a seat for me,'" Sara said.

Then GiGi segued into talking about Ana. "By the way, Ana and I
discussed your Angel talk with Chrissie. How important the Angels
were to her and how I knew, how important Ana's Angels were to her
too."

Suddenly GiGi was prompted to mention she was thinking of
changing the book's title.

"Why would you do that?" Sara gasped, "I thought 'The Angels
Made Me Do It' was writ in stone?"

"That's just what Ana said too until she heard the latest: 'Sara, Our
Angels and Me' and under that 'A Story of Friendship'," GiGi smiled
widely.

"I think I'd like to borrow your seat and try to absorb this," Sara
gasped again, "this 'suddenness' – that's all I can think of." Sara stopped

walking and then talking as she sat down on GiGi's cushioned walker seat.

GiGi said, "We'd better find a park bench. This friendship goes only so far. I can't push the walker with you on it."

The two friends started laughing and hugging each other.

"I really don't know what to say," Sara exclaimed "Except that I'm truly, highly honored. I don't believe I deserve to be included with you and our Angels, but wish it were so."

"Well, you can believe it," GiGi declared proudly. "If I'm lucky to have an editor eventually and the name has to be changed – it's still how I feel. I would try to keep that title."

"I'm embarrassed about all this," Sara blushed. "Now it's your turn. That's how I feel about us – but no book title to offer, only my love and encouragement to get back to your cane."

The women started laughing even harder again. People looked askance at the pair. Probably wondering about the great joke – whatever – that could make them laugh so hilariously.

But they knew, even as a little tearing managed to interrupt on occasion, it was a special day. After a while they relaxed.

GiGi asked Sara if she wanted any more, as she called it, "heavy stuff."

Sara said, "Sure. Bring it on."

"So, I told Ana how I felt even before that bad fall," GiGi said, referring to the fall she had that had caused her much pain and brought on the need for the walker. "But more so after it. How I felt something soft was wrapped around me and even being lifted a bit.

"Then Ana said that everyone was amazed how the worst things after the fall were painful bruises and needing stitches on a deep cut and the break in my nose, nothing broken otherwise. Ana said 'Your Angels were doing a great job for you.' I jokingly said 'Yeah, they want me to finish the book.' Then seriously, 'I feel very, very lucky. I certainly do believe in them.'"

"But did you tell her about your Angel 'journey'?" asked Sara.

"Yes, I started with: 'It always amazes me how we come from different backgrounds and still blend in our Fellowship. How our personal thoughts and feelings are never discussed unless within confidential groups," GiGi said, adding, "Then Ana said 'Unless someone wants to share those with everyone. There are always some who do.' I said 'That's true, but I'm usually not one of them. And it always amazes how we share so many beliefs, despite our different ages and various backgrounds like you and me.' Then Ana shared how she felt comfortable telling me about her boat trip, as she called it, to become a citizen. I thanked her for the sharing. I told her she could count on it being kept confidential."

GiGi continued, "Wanting to relate more about my Angel journey, I told her that after reading some books, I started to believe there was some Spirit, or whatever some people chose to call it, like God or Goddess or Mother Earth. How I also believed in the interconnectedness of all creatures and the earth. Then Ana told me she preferred to say 'God.' I said I knew that, but we respect each other's choices. We don't insist there is only one correct word or title. Then I told her of my other doubts, until one of my last therapists. She believed in Angels and introduced me to some interesting books. At the time, business was slow. I started to speak to one particular Angel. Whether it was my speaking to the Angel, a market change, whatever — business improved dramatically. I became an Angel believer."

Sara chuckled and said, "You know how some people would react to all that don't you?"

GiGi said firmly, "I sure do and don't care. It's worked for me all these years. It's like Roger's hand pushing me to delete the old book or the many occasions I've looked dozens of times for important papers and not found them, then been tugged just once more. Sure enough, a place I had searched many times before now revealed my long-sought papers. And the other night I needed to put some papers in the filing cabinet, but instead I took them out to the kitchen. There was the food I had forgotten to put in the fridge. It would have spoiled. How could I not believe?" GiGi said and then stopped as Sara was smiling widely at her and then GiGi added, "You really are a tease."

Sara responded "Madame GiGi is now a true Angel believer. She has finally joined our club."

The two women laughed, hugged and solemnly shook hands – just as they had done years ago when they first met at the Fellowship. They left the park together and headed home.

Over the next few days, GiGi kept thinking of recent as well as long ago letters and she wondered what was bothering her – Chrissie's letters, Sara's to her Mom and to ex-husband Jon, and all of a sudden she realized she wanted to share her special unwritten Gary "gift" letter with Sara.

The opportunity came up one day when they were, once again, sitting in Sara's living room.

"Sara, I was thinking of your letter to Jon the other day and wondered if you remembered it the way I do," said GiGi, talking about the letter Sara wrote to her ex-husband.

Sara looked puzzled and asked what brought that up.

"Well, remember how you wrote how unhappy you had been?" GiGi prompted, "How you didn't have sex for a few years because of his drinking? How you admitted to snooping and finding gay books under his mattress and…"

"Yeah and that confirmed what I had suspected," Sara recalled.

"The girls had told you he now had a partner," GiGi said. "Then you wished him and his partner well and hoped they could marry sometime and wished he had been able to be honest with you and himself years ago."

"Yeah, it seemed to be the only way I could forgive him," Sara said, adding "Then miracle of miracles he sent back a post card a week later with 'Me too.'"

"We had both remarked how similar some of our stories were," GiGi said.

Sara said, "Right, we are similar. By then he had paid me all the money owed for Sybil and when she was older he would take her for fun outings, until one day she refused to go without Sheila. Then he took both girls out. I wondered what Jon would think of all the good times I'd had since then and you couldn't resist remarking 'to each his own' and we laughed and laughed."

"It turned out to be so good because of your letter, Sara," GiGi said, adding "I know it wasn't easy as you wrote in the letter."

"You must be leading up to something," Sara deduced, "Come on, tell the rest of it."

"You're right on, as usual, and the reason is I wanted to share with you my mostly unwritten Gary letter and imagine this," GiGi said with a sly smile, "I even have it in my pocket."

They both laughed as GiGi took it out and started with "Gary, I want to thank you for your 'gift.'"

Suddenly Sheila came in, crying again, and saying "That funny lint is here again."

Sheila was obviously upset and both Sara and GiGi knew what was upsetting her. It had to do with something she kept seeing when she looked in a mirror. It was something unexplained, something strange and a little haunting. GiGi knew Sheila was going to need her mother Sara to comfort her.

So GiGi got up, folded the unfinished Gary letter and put it back in her pocket.

"This can wait," GiGi said. "It's been waiting for a long time already and we'll both enjoy another laugh another time."

GiGi went over to Sheila, told her she loved her, gave her a big hug and said "I'm willing to do anything to help. All you need do is ask."

Then GiGi did the same with Sara and then left her friend to deal with her daughter's distress, knowing they would call if they needed her.

Sara called after dinner to ask if GiGi wanted company. "Besides," she said "I would like to hear about Gary's so-called gift."

"I'd like to tell it too. It is how, what someone says and the other person hears, can be so different – resulting in an unexpected outcome. My ex-husband would have been surprised to discover he had given me a gift of any kind – but a gift it was," GiGi recalled.

"Well, does that mean you want to tell me the unwritten letter now?" Sara asked.

"Sure do, come over and we'll celebrate with a special dessert," GiGi said.

"Oh goody," Sara replied, "Well really two goodies in one night. That's a record. I'll be over shortly."

When Sara arrived she was wearing a lovely blue tunic over bright red tights. A white scarf with stars was tied in her hair. When she moved, her white chunky bracelets jangled.

"That outfit definitely makes a statement," GiGi observed.

"It's meant to represent liberty and freedom. Do you approve?" Sara asked.

GiGi applauded vigorously. "I sure do."

"OK," Sara said, "Now let's hear the fabulous unwritten letter."

When the women were seated on the sofa, Sara asked "Do we need tissues?"

GiGi laughed and said "Absolutely not. Relax and listen."

GiGi started with "Gary was in the hospital with some heart condition that needed medical supervision. I ended up in the same hospital on a different floor. The stress of our relationship had made my previous digestive problem flare up again. I didn't know if Gary knew I was in the hospital. After checking with his doctor, I guess he told him. Our doctors were aware of our relationship – or lack of one. But one doctor told me that Gary was going to need home care. I thought 'I need to work my usual 24/7 after I'm healthy again. But my husband would need care.'"

GiGi heard a little "uh-oh" from Sara but no more. Sara was obviously identifying with that feeling of having sick alcoholic husbands – soon to be sick alcoholic ex-husbands. GiGi remembered feeling her Angels getting ready to help. But as it turned out, help came from Gary himself.

"There's good coming, Sara – don't worry. I then asked for a Candy Striper to take me to Gary's room. I needed a wheelchair with its attachments since I was still on an intravenous drip. When we arrived at his room, Gary was ready, seated in a chair near the window. The young woman disappeared tactfully and we were alone. I started to tell Gary what his doctor had said. I told him I needed to start back to work when I got home but since he needed home care I would be willing to take time off from work until he was better and he interrupted with 'Forget it – as far as I'm concerned you're dead' and turned away. I guess he turned away. I was so excited I almost leaped out of the wheelchair. I called out to be taken back to my room. My nurses must have been startled to hear my laughter and to see me jumping up and down with glee. Those wonderful words, they were meant to hurt me, but they were the most beautiful ones I could have heard. I had my freedom – what a release."

Sara exclaimed, "I knew my outfit meant we celebrate."

"Yes," GiGi continued "He could have had a wife to care for him. After all you didn't leave a sick husband. That's what wives were expected to do no matter the relationship."

Sara said, "Yeah, no matter the relationship? I'm glad times are different now."

"But he gave me a gift instead," GiGi said again, "My glorious freedom and now I want to thank him for it – in my previously unwritten, unsent letter: 'Gary, thank you for my freedom.'"

Sara let out a long sigh. "All I can say is what a beautiful story. And how about that special dessert you were talking about. I know it's our delicious coffee ice cream to celebrate your freedom."

"Well, it's another freedom type of thing," GiGi said and then she heard Sara say, 'Uh, oh. Now what, another one of your healthy foods? I can hardly wait."

"Skip the sarcasm and listen to my plan," GiGi said, "We need to fool our bodies into enjoying something else besides ice cream. It's adding inches and pounds to us as we speak."

"Not as I speak, maybe as you do," Sara said. "Oh well, you might as well finish telling me the whole plan, otherwise we'll never eat anything tonight."

"I decided to try cherry Jell-O with a dollop of yogurt as substitutes," GiGi stated, pleased with herself. "I know it isn't our coffee flavor but it actually is pretty good. I think our bodies will enjoy something less fattening than our usual ice cream."

"It still isn't the coffee flavor that I love so much," Sara pouted. "But bring on what you have. Let's try it."

When GiGi brought in pretty glass dishes filled with the substitute dessert, Sara suddenly exclaimed, "How about turning on the TV. 'The Closer' is starting another series. It's one of my favorite programs. Maybe that can help me enjoy our newest dessert."

"I think you'll be surprised," GiGi suggested.

"Say, you're right. It is nice and the flavor's pretty good too. You've hit the jackpot with this one.'" Sara stated after her initial taste. "Besides I have to agree it's less fattening." And so it was.

CHAPTER 9

ANA SHARES A STORY ABOUT VICTOR'S MOTHER

One evening Sara, GiGi and their friend Ana were relaxing on their favorite park bench and enjoying the soft summer breezes. A handsome couple passed them dressed in beautifully colored clothing that seemed to be some kind of native dress. It looked to be flowing cotton with all manner of bright colored threads running through it. The many colors were eye-catching, as was the sparkling jewelry worn by the young woman.

After they passed, Ana said, "That reminds me of the young Muslim Lori has been dating the last few weeks. She really likes him."

Sara nodded, "She's met a lot of Muslims in school and the hospital, hasn't she?"

"Of course, but this time she really, really likes him," Ana declared.

"Does that bother you Ana?" GiGi asked.

"Of course not, but it does bother some of her friends when they all go out together," Ana replied.

Sara asked, "What do they do?"

"Well they make snide remarks, very quietly, but Lori hears them and so does her boyfriend," said Ana.

"What does she say when that happens?" asked GiGi.

"She's didn't know how to handle it. I told her to make her friends understand that she will not tolerate those remarks and to remember how they felt when other people made similar remarks about them," Ana said.

"Did they?" asked Sara.

"Of course, Sara," answered Ana. "Remember the atmosphere when I first came to our school as the nurse. For a while it was pretty uncomfortable until you and a few others spoke up for me. Still some people feel differently even though I was born here and have no accent. I can feel it when they talk to me."

"What is Lori going to do if her friends continue to be nasty?" asked Sara.

"Well she is hoping they will understand and remember and change for the better, of course. She would give up these so-called friends if they continued. They wouldn't be the kind of people she wanted to be friends with," Ana said rather proudly.

"Sounds like your Lori is still the same young woman we have always admired," GiGi said.

"I agree," Sara declared. "That's why we always thought she was so special. A lot of it is due to you Ana. You have been a great mother to her and Victor and it must have been hard while your husband was sick and then when he died and you were a single mom."

"Thanks," said Ana. "But my two children are just the best possible, and so much of it came from Victor Sr. too, even when he was ill. He did as much as he could to be a father like he had. His father would never stand for intolerant behavior and abuse. He was quite a guy."

"Bet Victor would have liked Lori's Muslim friend if she and you do. He must be special if you and Lori like him so much," GiGi added.

"He is and we'll just wait and see how this relationship will turn out. As long as she's happy – that's it for me too," Ana declared.

They all nodded and as they were leaving the park, everyone expressed their hopes that all would be well for Lori and her new boyfriend.

That evening as she was alone in her apartment, GiGi thought about Ana and the time they were waiting for Sara and the topic of letters and the book came up again. They were seated in their favorite pizzeria. Sara had told them her doctor's appointment might make her late.

Out of the blue Ana said, "I just remembered about a special letter."

GiGi asked, "Was it one you sent?"

"No, but someone did many years ago and I know you will want to have it in the book," Ana replied.

"Ana, you know how much I want all kinds of sent and unsent letters – you bet I want it. Well, up to a point anyhow, it will have to make sense," GiGi stipulated.

"Oh it makes sense all right and I know Sara will agree on this," Ana said.

GiGi and Ana had been waiting a bit impatiently at this point. Sara was more than half an hour late. Then Sara came rushing in. "Sorry to be so late – the traffic was terrible."

"What's the doctor's report?" Ana and GiGi asked nearly simultaneously.

"Oh, everything is fine. OK to continue – same as usual – even with my kind of yummy foods we have here. So what did you order?" Sara asked eagerly.

"We waited for you," GiGi and Ana said again at the same time. Just then their usual waitress came up.

"Need a few minutes?" the waitress asked.

"Nope. You know us, the usual half regular tomato with extra sauce and half with veggies and iced tea for all," GiGi said as she ordered.

As the trio settled back after the order was taken, Ana started her letter story.

"Lori and I were talking the other night about the time her father wouldn't let her and young Victor visit his mother's house. Don't know how or why it came up but there it was," Ana said.

GiGi nodded, "Somehow it always does."

Ana continued, "Oh yes, I do remember. We were talking about

Victor's will and some old papers he had left. He had established bank accounts for Lori and Victor for their schooling, years before. They were all bundled in with other papers – securely wrapped with rubber bands – and stuffed in a shiny tin box that had held cigars years before."

"Was the letter inside?" GiGi asked.

"Yes, it was from his mother," Ana revealed.

This time Sara couldn't help interrupting. She said, "Just like my Aunt Rose and Nana. Oops sorry Ana – this is your story. Sorry. So what happened?"

"Well it was a long letter apologizing for anything she had said or done to him. She said she loved him and that whatever it was, she never meant to hurt him," Ana recalled.

Ana continued, "Then he left it out one day, sort of forgetting to put all the papers away. You know how it goes, I shouldn't have looked at it, but of course he wanted me to see it. He knew how I felt about the estrangement and that I wanted the children to visit their grand-mother. But his answer was always: 'It's between my mother and me.' And he would never tell me why he was so angry. I had told him before and repeated again: 'I take the children to see your mother when you are not home. There is no reason for them to be kept apart except for your stubbornness in not even talking to your mother about whatever is bothering you. I don't do it often because it's hard traveling with all the kids' stuff but at least she does see them once in a while. And I always bring her pictures or mail them to her when there's a special occasion. I think you have turned being some kind of victim into being a bully.' He gave me a long look, said nothing just picked up the letter and left the room."

The letter said:

Dear son,

Since you haven't responded to the other letters (and I know you've received them) there is no sense in continuing a one-sided dialogue except for this last letter.

You are so like your father who would never allow intolerance in our home. You were always encouraged to bring home any and all of your friends. Many times they would tell me, in a quiet confidential way, how welcome they felt in our home. How their families would be rude to their guests and how they were discouraged from bringing them home.

There were also times when they would confide about some hurt that had occurred and would ask my opinion on how to handle it because they couldn't talk with their parents about it.

Over the years, your father and I were so proud that you could talk with us about anything that bothered you. We had conversations.

But now, it seems there is something that has caused you to stop talking with me.

I don't think your father would have waited this long—he would have confronted you to 'have it out.' I have waited because of little Victor and Lori. I kept thinking you would change your mind and let me see them. As it turns out, Ana has brought them to my house. She has shared that she tells you when she does so but she isn't comfortable doing it.

So, in this last letter I will repeat and repeat that I love you and that what happened between us is something that was never meant to hurt you. Never would I do anything deliberately to hurt you in any way—I love you too much.

I realize that whatever did happen between us may have made you believe I was bullying or abusing you. Whatever, it must have made you feel a victim. That is why you are now depriving all of us of having a normal family relationship.

Perhaps you don't realize it, but you have now become a bully by doing this. If, whatever was done to you is too painful to talk about, at least let us take a chance on letting go and moving forward. I will let go of the pain of not seeing my grandchildren in a normal family relationship if you can also move forward.

I love you Victor. I'm so proud of how like your father you are in every respect—except this one. Little Victor and Lori, Ana and you, and

I deserve to return to a normal family relationship. I pray you and I will be able to move forward and may God bless us all.
Your Mother

Then Ana said, "I didn't know it at the time that young Victor had told his father about a trip to see grandma and how she gave him a big birthday present but he couldn't bring it home – the fort was too heavy – and why didn't she bring it here? I don't know what or why or when, but one day his mother called to invite us over for a family party. I relayed the message to Victor hoping he had changed and he had. He said, 'Sure we will all go and tell her we'll bring the wine.' I don't know when, or even if, they had talked things out. Somehow circumstances and that letter did the trick. So you see that sent letter was successful and I don't think Victor would mind if you put it in the book."

GiGi said, "Thanks for sharing, Ana. It must have been hard visiting and telling him you went. After all, a wife is supposed to support her husband."

"Well I have mixed feelings when the circumstances make it necessary to take other steps," Ana explained. "It was hard though and I never concealed anything from him."

Sara said nothing and seemed saddened rather than pleased at the eventual outcome.

Ana said to her, "I thought you'd be glad of the ending."

"Oh I am," Sara said, 'It's just that it brought up my Nana and Aunt Rose, and that was never resolved. Nana sent letters by the bushel – always saying how she loved Aunt Rose and would never have deliberately wanted to hurt her and pleading to be allowed to see her grandchildren. She showed me many of them and some had tear stains. I'm not sure from me or Nana. In any case, Aunt Rose would not discuss it. It was always with the 'It's between me and Nana.' But then she wouldn't talk with Nana about it either. Nana never knew what terrible thing she had done, or said, that would make her daughter so angry."

Ana said softly, and it seemed sadly, "It sounds like your Aunt Rose was prosecutor, judge and jury, and never revealed the charges to your Nana. I guess she must have always wondered what it could have been — and if she could have changed whatever it was."

Sara said, "That's exactly right. What terrible thing could have happened to make her be so hated that she couldn't even see her own grandchildren? It was awful."

Their waitress stopped at the table and asked her usual "Is there anything else?"

The three looked at each other and GiGi said, "No." But then she hastily added "It's not you or the restaurant — it's just us."

They all sighed. Someone said "No dessert this time, just the check." Then they left.

CHAPTER 10

SARA SHARES A BIG SECRET

"I need lots of chocolate," was Sara's cry at 8:30 that night. Earlier they had listened to Ana's story and then Sara's and it had been very emotional.

"Well, I just happen to have a box of chocolate cookies. Will that do?" GiGi asked. "Should I bring them over?"

"Yes, oh yes. I have tried every hiding place – hiding from me that is – and can't find a single one," Sara said desperately.

"OK, I'll come by shortly and we can binge," GiGi responded, "We may regret it later but for now it should do the trick."

On the way, GiGi stopped at the corner deli and found coffee ice cream – not her favorite brand but so what? She also picked up some peanut butter cookies. They would be welcome too, she knew.

"Oh, I'm so glad to see the grocery bag. Well, you too, of course," Sara said as she almost ripped the bag from GiGi's hands.

GiGi called after her, "Don't forget to leave some for me. The messenger always deserves at least that."

Sara grinned, "After me, messenger," as she took down some bowls and small plates. "We are about to binge and have some memories disappear for a while and how about some TV too?"

GiGi responded, "Sounds just right to me."

As they settled down on Sara's comfy sofa with their goodies – watching short pieces of ballet and opera on the one station that showed them with no advertising. It's on during the day as well as the evening, interspersed with lots of educational programs.

"This is so relaxing and fortifying," said Sara. "Well, comforting is a better word. Thanks for coming over with the goodies. I just needed some TLC."

"I guess we both needed it after Nana's story," was GiGi's response.

A few minutes later, out of the blue, Sara asked GiGi, "Don't you get depressed with all those stories and knowing someone else has surely gone through the same thing – what a world!"

"Well I have been called Little Miss Sunshine on occasion but sometimes I think it's a bit mocking," GiGi said.

Sara said, "I'm not sure because you usually think your glass is half full and I know how many times people have been helped with your pearls of wisdom."

"You are too kind," GiGi responded, "But I can tell you of a really depressing time and how Max helped me out of it."

"Max? Who is he, another boyfriend that you met in the newspaper ads?" Sara asked.

GiGi thought about the brown mixed breed collie with white around his eyes and throat. She saw his lavish hair that looked so beautiful especially along the ridge on his back. She had gotten him from a friend who was fed up with his chewing everything including her shoes. GiGi remembered how she had stepped in and kept the friend from giving this cute little guy away because of the chewing problem and how initially he chewed GiGi's things too. Eventually he did learn not to chew everything, but mostly GiGi remembered how he was so much attuned to her moods and how he would care for her.

"Nope, he was a dear brown furry friend who would not allow me to stay in bed or mope around the house. He did the original tugging. Guess the Angels put him up to it and I didn't even know it. I owe him a special thank you letter and will send it to the great animal heaven wherever it is," GiGi declared, about the dog who was such a good friend to her.

Sara said seriously, "I don't picture you so depressed that you would just stay in bed."

"You can believe it and he would not leave me alone. He would stay close to my bed and look at me with those soft brown eyes saying 'I need you to get up and take me out for a walk – or at least get me into the fenced yard,'" GiGi recalled.

"I remember," Sara said, "About the yard and how the donkey from across the street would come over and Max – now I remember his name – and the donkey would touch noses through the wire fence – and then you would call someone to come over to take the donkey home."

"Yes, and watching the two of them always helped," GiGi said. "They were so cute. Really not cuddly but just cute together and I could sort of laugh a bit."

Sara said, "Isn't it amazing how pets, in particular, sense when something is wrong and help us to make it right without any scolding or pushing. Well tugging is OK. I'd call your Max an earth-bound Angel dog wouldn't you?"

GiGi answered, "Absolutely. And I'll write him a letter so he can share it with the other Angel dogs."

Then GiGi thought about her other dear animal companion, her sweet little 6-pound cat who was so protective of her as well. She recalled how fierce that little cat would become as she puffed herself up when she felt she needed to protect the house and how every time GiGi passed by her she would raise her head and "speak" to her human friend. GiGi said, "I can't forget my dear, sweet Cat-Cat. She would cuddle up on my lap or in bed—always purring, always loving. She didn't tug at me – she let Max do that job. But her acceptance and love always helped get me on my feet again."

Then GiGi added, "So between chocolate, Max, Cat-Cat and TV you seem to be all cheered up."

Sara said, "For now at least."

Then Sara chuckled, "And you would say 'And so it was'."

The two women shared their usual hugs and said their good nights, both feeling a bit better from the food and company.

Even though the night before, Sara and GiGi had binged their way into feeling a bit better, the next morning it seemed something still wasn't right. GiGi noticed right away when Sara called that something seemed to be heavy in the air.

She started by saying "Thanks for always being willing to lend me an ear. I hope you won't judge me too harshly when you hear this story."

"Oh Sara," GiGi said.

Sara interrupted with, "I need to not get dressed. If you wouldn't mind, how about coming to my place?"

GiGi immediately said, "That's fine. I'm ready to go out and will be there in a few minutes."

GiGi would have done anything to help Sara with whatever was troubling her. "It must be something tremendous," GiGi thought. "Oh poor Sara, I hope she doesn't have some terrible disease or the girls – whatever, I'll be there for them."

When GiGi reached Sara's apartment, Sara was waiting but not in her usual beautiful nightclothes. She was pulled together with different colors, styles – like a hodgepodge – a long purple scarf barely holding it together. It was evident she was upset.

GiGi hugged her and said "I'm ready when you are and know I will always love you—no matter what."

Sara led them to the family room and put a tissue box on the sofa between them.

"I'll need them," she said and started with, "Way back, when I was recently divorced from Jon, I was going to school, working part time and raising Sybil with some occasional help from my mom. I had a very close friend, Leila, who had been most supportive when I was getting my divorce. She was engaged and planned to be married the following year. I was fond of her and her fiancé, Daniel, and helped her plan their wedding."

"In the meantime," Sara continued, "I was having a rough time financially. Jon wasn't always on time with child support. I didn't want my mom to know how tough it was. I had too much pride."

Then Sara stopped. After a bit, GiGi asked if this was time for some tea and Sara eagerly agreed.

GiGi and Sara sat quietly for a few minutes, slowly sipping their tea – each wrapped in their own thoughts. Trying to relax wasn't easy. The air crackled with all kinds of emotions.

After a while, Sara turned. With tears in her eyes she said, "I don't think I can finish this just yet. Would you mind if I stop now? I need to be by myself."

GiGi said, "Sara, please do whatever is right for you. Know I'm always available for sharing or quiet times. I love you and support you, no matter what."

They hugged and GiGi left. She noticed Sara had not said her usual "promise" which meant she would continue her story as soon as possible. All GiGi could do was wait.

The next day, Sara called to say she was feeling better. She wanted to continue her story. "Would today be OK – same time and place?" Sara asked and GiGi readily agreed.

This time when GiGi arrived it was more like the usual Sara – she wore a pretty floral top, that GiGi liked, and long turquoise skirt to complement it, plus her usual Birkenstocks. Her hair was neatly pulled back and held with a big barrette. She seemed ready to do battle, GiGi thought – to get the story out.

The two hugged and Sara said, "Thank you for understanding yesterday. You were the only person I had ever told anything. Now it's time to reveal the whole story. That's because you are special and I know you will understand."

GiGi felt flattered but said nothing and waited.

Sara began, "Well Leila always wanted a son like Daniel. They tried many times but she was able to conceive only once. Sadly she was unable to carry the fetus for more than a couple of months. Other than that one time she wasn't able to conceive. Finally Leila decided it was too emotionally and physically draining each time. She convinced Daniel to store some sperm. They could try again or maybe have a surrogate mother carry the fetus to bring her the son she desired."

Sara continued, "And then tragically, Daniel was killed in a terrible auto accident. After a few months Leila decided she still wanted Daniel's baby and she insisted that I help her. She knew things were difficult financially for me. She proposed I become the surrogate mom with Daniel's sperm and my eggs. She would pay me $15,000 but we would never reveal the complete story to Daniel's family. They lived in England, were fond of her and were as devastated as she at his death. He and his family were quite wealthy and Daniel had left everything he had to Leila. She was in a position to do whatever she wanted financially."

Sara continued, "I kept refusing, saying she should have someone else. But she insisted it had to be me. So, with the carrot of $15,000 in front of me, I agreed. And the story for the world, or whoever needed to know it, would be that Daniel's sperm and Leila's eggs would be carried by me. At the ripe age of 32, I never thought any further. What could happen that would destroy that story? Leila would have her desired son, and Sybil and I would have an easier life. So the arrangements were made. My pregnancy was easy and successful. Too successful as it turned out because I had twins – a boy and a girl."

Then GiGi let out a slight "Uh oh."

Sara said "Yeah, uh oh doubled. I had no one to talk to. My mom thought I was still that loose teenager. What was I to do since Leila wanted only the boy? There was no way I could think of raising another baby – a single mother."

GiGi was thinking what a difficult situation when Sara said, "In any case, it was settled for us in a very strange way. You know how it can happen, like when babies are sent home from the hospital with the wrong parents. Mysteriously, on the girl's birth certificate it listed me as the mother. Leila was listed as the mother on the boy's. Don't ask. It was a miracle."

Sara went on, "At this point Leila was firm about not wanting a girl that might not look like her. There was no convincing her otherwise. The result was she paid me $20,000 more and said she would always support 'our' little girl. What could I do? I had carried this baby nine months. It was tough having to give up the boy. But now I would keep the little girl. All that moving and kicking, that life – there is something to be said about postpartum emotions and I agreed to that whole mad scheme."

It definitely was time for more than tea. Sara brought out some wine. They both gulped a few times, stopped and put down their wine glasses. They embraced again and again, stopping only to wipe away their tears.

Then Sara announced, "I chose to call her Sheila because that was close to the name Leila. She knows only that I'm her mother – that her father was killed in an auto accident before we could be married. But that piece you knew, GiGi, that Sheila's father had died."

GiGi looked at her friend saying "Oh Sara I didn't know the half of it did I? How tough it must have been for you." GiGi reached out, gave Sara another hug and said "I love and support you in every way I can."

Sara nodded. "This is just the beginning and I know I will need you and your love and support. Thank you in advance," Sara said as she returned GiGi's hug.

GiGi asked, "Are you thinking this has something to do with the lint?"

"Yes," Sara said, "I feel that lint Sheila sees in the mirror every once in a while has something to do with Leila and little Daniel. I can't shake that feeling. And the most difficult part is that neither Sybil nor Sheila knows this whole story. They only know that Sheila's father died."

"Are you thinking about telling them now because the lint is showing up more frequently?" asked GiGi.

"No, it is quite the opposite. I want to know why the lint and then tell them," responded Sara. "Leila and Daniel—he's big Daniel now— may even be the kind of people who could harm Sheila. I'm not sure which is the right way to go. All I do know is I'm frightened and don't want to scare the girls too."

GiGi didn't know what to say except Sara had all her love and support. She needed to think about it – and maybe her Angels would have suggestions. The two friends hugged each other tearfully several more times. Finally they had to part and GiGi left Sara with her terrible dilemma – which she now shared. It would be a while before they talked more about this. Both women needed some time to be with their thoughts about it all. It was a lot to consider.

CHAPTER 11

GIGI ASKS VICTOR ABOUT BLOGGING

A few days after Sara's story, GiGi was sitting alone in her apartment looking inquisitively over the daily ads for the newest technological gadgets. Technology intrigued her but she had no idea where to start with it all.

"I've decided to take the plunge," GiGi thought. "I've decided to take the chance and hope that not too many people will laugh at me and to finally ask someone to explain blogging to me."

She chuckled. "I expect 'Welcome to the 21st century' or some such remark like 'Why do you want to know?'"

Then she remembered Ana had told her about her son Victor. He had offered, after hearing about GiGi hating to ask people for rides – to give GiGi rides on his motorcycle. Well, actually he would ask a friend to borrow his bike that had an extra seat. He would take GiGi, no charge, wherever she wanted to go. When Ana told GiGi about this, she teared up a bit. GiGi said she'd like to meet with him. Then GiGi was even more eager when Ana said how good Victor was on the computer.

So finally this day GiGi called on Victor for help. It was a Saturday and Victor came prepared to offer rides. Instead he was greeted by GiGi with "What can you tell me about blogging?"

"You sound like my Mom," he said, adding, "And why – I hope you don't mind my asking – do you want to know?"

GiGi explained about her book about bullying and also writing letters to help heal things between people or even to just heal one's self.

She told him how she hoped to spread the information that people could help themselves by writing letters but not necessarily sending them.

"Yeah, I know. My Mom told me about Grandma's letter. You know the whole story about my Dad and stuff and how it worked out," Victor said.

"So you can understand how it can help," GiGi said, explaining, "But people have to know how. I heard about blogging and thought, maybe I could try it."

"Sure. I can show you how on your computer," Victor agreed, then asked, "Uh, do you have one?"

GiGi laughed and pointed to the other wall. "There it is – waiting to be used."

"It's OK with me if you'd like to start now," Victor said. "I have some time now, so we could get started."

"That would be great," GiGi agreed.

Victor sat down in front of the computer and asked GiGi if she "knew Excel."

"Well I've heard of it," GiGi said, "But, no, I don't know how to use it."

Suddenly, Victor smiled and asked GiGi a few more computer-related questions.

"You really don't know very much, do you?" Victor smiled.

GiGi had to admit that was true.

"Well, I'll be glad to help you, as my Mom's friend. But for now I'll show you anything but 'blogging.' You really need more first," Victor stipulated.

"You mean you could help me get organized with my stories and players for the book?" GiGi asked excitedly.

"Sure. I'd be glad to," Victor replied.

"Well, if you do, I'll even put you in the book," GiGi offered.

"Really, you'd put my name and everything?" Victor seemed excited too.

"Not really – but a story about what you're doing to help – do you mind?" GiGi asked.

"Nah, that's OK. I'll know it's really me anyhow," Victor said with a note of satisfaction.

They made a deal. Victor would do this as a friend. But GiGi also wanted to pay him something for his time and expertise. He agreed she could help by paying for some things he needed for his motorcycle.

They struck the deal and Victor left GiGi to head off to work.

Several days later, as if the theme of new things and new trends was still in the air, GiGi and Sara were eating at their favorite diner when suddenly nearby came some very loud voices.

"Comfort Sex, is that what they call it now?" the first voice exploded. "Shh," came the second voice in the diner. Sara and GiGi obviously were the unwilling neighbors in the next booth. They looked at each other, continued eating, and waited for the next outburst. It came quickly.

"Why would you even consider going out with him – this worm after he proposed this – this – unspeakable thing?" The reply came back softly, and defensively, "He didn't exactly propose it – just mentioned he saw an article in the papers."

"Huh, just like him. Can't come out and say 'how about it, kiddo?' It's just like him," Voice number one kept mumbling. Voice number two quietly suggested they drop the subject and leave. As usual, there was the intense discussion of who ordered what and how much tip to leave.

GiGi murmured, "Why don't they just split everything?"

Sara agreed, "Like we do, it's so easy that way as long as one person doesn't always order more expensive items or drink a lot more wine."

"Yeah, guess you're right – but at least we don't have to dine with her," GiGi said quietly, tossing her head slightly in the direction of voice number one.

After the noisy diners left, Sara told GiGi that she had seen the article too and it sounded like it might be interesting. She said quickly "But let's discuss it in another place, don't you think?"

GiGi agreed that was a good idea.

Later, seated on their favorite park bench, Sara told GiGi how she had tried comfort sex with no strings attached, years ago when she was first divorced. She reminded GiGi that it was now called "Friends-with-Benefits." They agreed that was a more appropriate name. Sara said she became friends with one particular man and turned to him for guidance and help when things became tough. Over time, they had sex and it made her feel like she was desirable after Jon's avoidance of her and sex. At the time, she didn't realize that her ex-husband's attitude toward sex was something he couldn't help. In any case, she enjoyed being cuddled by this new friend and the whole relationship.

At this point, GiGi added "I had a similar arrangement. It was fun too."

Sara smiled and continued her story. She and her friend stopped when she became a surrogate mom. She wanted to be sure about Leila's baby and took no chances, though her friend had always used protection.

GiGi asked "Did you ever want to marry again?"

Sara said that was not what she wanted. Luckily she found some-one who felt the same way – it was comfortable for both.

Again GiGi smiled and said "Me too. But what about the other men you've dated over the years? I thought you wanted a non-com-mitted relationship?"

Sara laughed and said, "Yes, that was then. Now I'm looking for my soul mate and commitment. One of these days, he'll be there and then I can stop looking. It may take a few years. Anyhow, look at the committed relationships between octogenarians we read about. I'm willing to wait for the right one." Then she giggled and said, "And don't forget – 92 is not too old either, GiGi."

GiGi laughed and said, "While we are waiting, here's to Comfort Sex with a vibrator, in the meantime."

And they both chuckled.

CHAPTER 12
NOISY NEIGHBORS MOVE IN

A few days later, GiGi and Sara went on one of their brisk walks in the park. "Whew," said GiGi. "Let's stop for a few minutes."

While she and GiGi sat on their favorite park bench people watching, pigeon feeding and just in general relaxing, Sara suddenly complained "My new neighbors are making a lot of noise."

"Whooo," GiGi said with exhaustion, "I'm not used to all this, even with the walker. How did you talk me into this early morning, brisk walk?"

Sara laughed, "It's good for you to relax. You spend too much time at that computer working on your book."

"Then why bring up your noisy neighbors right now? Let's just relax," GiGi said.

"No can do," said Sara "I have to get this out and you are my designated listener – like it or not."

"Well I could get up, if possible," GiGi retorted, "And briskly – well slowly – walk away and..."

"I know you too well," Sara said "You want to know what's happening and wouldn't miss this for the world."

Then it was GiGi's time to laugh. "You're right because I've always been in on all your gossip."

"Well I sent them a letter, very polite, asking them to please turn down the TV," Sara said, "And they never responded at all – just kept the sound loud as usual."

"These are new people – right?" GiGi asked. "Did you ever meet them?"

"Well no. I was on vacation when they moved in and they pretty much keep to themselves. That's why I sent that nice letter welcoming them to the neighborhood. " Sara explained, adding "Never knew when they would be home and didn't really want to have a confrontation. I thought the polite letter would do it."

"Obviously it didn't work. How about just going over with a small plant or something and try talking to them?" GiGi suggested.

"Guess I'll have to," Sara said. Then she let that subject go and launched into something about a newspaper report that school nurses see bullies and victims more often than other classmates.

"What brought that up?" GiGi asked. "You certainly seem to be on some kind of mission of reporting, changing, complaining or something this morning. Have I listed everything?"

"Yes, you have and I guess I'm upset because I heard from Chrissie. You remember my young friend on her train ride to Florida—I met her coming back from Vermont. She thinks her uncle and brother will get away with light sentences and not get what they deserve. They seem to have been able to make a deal and she and the other victims are really angry and hurt."

GiGi blurted out "Oh Sara that's awful. After all they've been through. What do they plan to do?"

"Chrissie didn't know but she doesn't plan to be quiet about it — that's for sure."

"Is there any way we can help from this distance?" GiGi offered. "Does she need some money to hire an attorney or something?"

"I'll ask her," Sara said. "And I'll tell her we want to help and for her to keep us informed, OK?"

"Sounds like the only thing right now." GiGi said. "And tell her to get her Angels working on it too."

Sara nodded and said "Will do."

Then the two friends left the park and headed home.

It was two days later when GiGi picked up the phone to hear Sara exclaim, "You won't believe this."

"Oh Sara luv, I learned a long time ago, when you say that, I will definitely believe in the unbelievable, now what?" GiGi asked.

"Well you remember my complaints about my new neighbors and you suggested I go over with a plant?"

"You mean you actually took my advice and went over?" GiGi asked, chuckling a bit. "You did so without even kicking and screaming. You actually went?"

"OK, OK, now listen and don't you dare say a word," Sara warned, adding "Maybe till the very end."

GiGi settled back on her rocker and waited. This sounded like it would be good.

Sara started with the pretty little hyacinth plant she bought and how she waited until the postman came, knocked on the neighbors' door and then left. It seemed someone might be home this time so she rang the bell.

"This is the part that's interesting," Sara declared. "A young Asian woman opened the door and said they were not interested in buying anything, except she said it with a strong accent. It took me a while to understand what she was trying to say."

Suddenly, Sara explained, there was a loud voice saying "Have the person come in."

The young woman motioned for Sara to come in. She was escorted into a large, sunlit living room where she saw an elderly gentleman seated on a huge couch.

"Well, rather he was on the couch and covered with several beautiful shawls. It seemed a bit warm for that – but he looked comfortable," Sara recounted.

"I said 'How do you do? I'm your neighbor and I brought you a plant.' The gentleman said 'Do sit down and please excuse if I don't get up.' He gestured toward the ottoman next to him," Sara continued.

"'Oh please,' I said, 'I just wanted to follow up on my letter requesting you to turn down the loud TV sound and...' Then before I could finish the rest of it he asked me to speak up. He explained he was hard of hearing and also did not see too well."

By this time, Sara said she was embarrassed and didn't know what to say and he went on: "You will have to excuse me if I do not follow your words but my son will be able to talk with you when he returns from his business trip next week. I like to listen to the TV and radio because it is company while he's away. My aide speaks little English. When my son David returns, we will look for a more permanent assistant, as I like to call my aide."

By this time, Sara said she was ready do anything, say anything and leave as quickly and gracefully as possible. The elderly gentleman continued with "I'm a retired Rabbi and my son brought me here to live near him and his wife. They want me to be comfortable in my own home with an assistant."

Sara said she nodded and understood and said that she would call on him when his son was available and left after getting his phone number.

"Sara, he must be very lonely to tell you so many things so quickly," GiGi said.

"Oh I'm sure he is and I plan to go over again even before his son returns," Sara stated. "He was such a charmer and he needs some company. In fact you can come too."

"There you go," GiGi said smiling, "Always willing to share the good times. But yes, if it's convenient when you go, I'd love to come too."

"Incidentally he told me his name was Rappaport – Rabbi Rappaport." Sara shared.

"OK if I chuckle now?" GiGi asked. "You were all prepared for whatever and you found a new friend. Maybe the TV noise isn't so annoying now?"

"Yes, and just think, he fits right in with the priest and his wife who live two floors above. What we need is a retired minister and the building will be renamed Heavenly Quarters or some such," Sara said with a smile.

GiGi smiled too. "Funny you should mention that, Sara, because I believe that there is one just waiting to be introduced to you and somehow he or she will come here too."

"No joking. I just happen to know someone who knows a minister and she could come to visit," said Sara, "It would be interesting to see them all together. Think I'll work on it and wouldn't the Angels love that?"

GiGi liked the idea too.

CHAPTER 13

A RABBI, A PRIEST AND A REVEREND WALK INTO A PARTY...

Sara had invited Rabbi Rappaport and his son, David and daughter-in-law, Kristen, as well as the priest – still wasn't sure what denomination – and his wife, plus an old friend Rev. Emily Jonsen along with GiGi, of course, as wine provider and general all-around-helper. By this time, everyone there knew the priest and his wife were Father Pat and Marie – the possibly retired, whatever faith couple and their grown son, James, who was in town just for the weekend. Sara had been asked if that was all right since he was here for such a short time and wanted to meet some of his parents' neighbors.

Sara agreed as usual – always eager to meet new people – and there they were gabbing away – munching on cheese tidbits and enjoying GiGi's fine wine choices, when Marie suddenly said, "Pat and I thought it might be uncomfortable for some of you not knowing exactly who we are and trying not to say anything improper. We know, we've been there ourselves."

Well that certainly was bold GiGi thought.

Marie continued, "We plan to live here for a long while and want to have neighbors who will feel comfortable with us and us with you. Anyhow that's it. So ask your questions and it's OK. We're used to it."

"Well I was wondering since you mentioned 'Mass' to GiGi, whether that was Catholic or Episcopal Mass," said Sara, as GiGi had told her of her previous conversation with Father Pat.

"I think it might be better if I start at the beginning," said Father Pat. "I met Marie when her husband passed away unexpectedly 33 years ago. She was Catholic and he had been Episcopal and I was his priest. I counseled Marie and her family, and over time my family became close friends with them. When my wife died 25 years ago, they were there for us as well. About two or three years after that, Marie and I realized we were falling in love and decided to talk it over with our families and try for their blessing. They were all excited about combining the families and we were married November 10th."

"No dear, it was the 12th," said Marie with a twinkle in her eye. "I think he just says that so I'll correct him."

"Right," said Father Pat, "Then I'll know you remember the correct date."

They all chuckled.

"But what church do you attend?" asked Sara.

"Oh yes, I need to finish the story. I had been thinking of changing over to the Catholic Church, and after Marie and I were married for a few years, I did convert to Catholicism and was one of very few married priests at the time."

"I know two," said Rev. Emily Jonsen, and she thanked Pat and Marie for sharing their story, adding, "They sort of followed the way you two did, romance and all."

David said, "My father's been nodding his head. He also knew two married priests; maybe they're the same ones. He'll talk with you about it later."

So the afternoon went along, remembering old mutual friends, telling about the many joint meetings of religious leaders especially to combat bullying and bigotry in their towns. It sounded like a political gathering at times, and Sara and GiGi just listened and tried to absorb everything. The two friends would have much to discuss themselves later on.

Then Rev. Emily said she had heard that GiGi was writing a book about bullying and was wondering why GiGi had chosen that subject.

"There seems to be even more bullying and harassment than ever," GiGi said, "Or at least it's more evident because of all the electronic equipment available – TV, Facebook, Twitter, etc. I wanted to help people be aware of this and if they were abused to know how they could help heal themselves by writing letters."

"I've heard of that," said Rev. Emily. "But how does it help?"

"Writing about the incident," GiGi explained, "Even if one doesn't send the actual letter, letting the bully know how you feel about the abuse, seems to help people recover."

"How interesting," Father Pat said, "I have stories I could tell you. Maybe we should get together some time and chat."

"I guess I shouldn't ask to set an appointment now," GiGi said, "But I am always interested in hearing new stories."

David said, "Look out Father Pat; I have a feeling you'll end up in the book."

"I might not be able to resist if I think it could help," GiGi declared.

Then the Rabbi spoke about the one day a year Jews are supposed to atone for their sins, Yom Kippur. He slyly asked, "I wonder how many letters will be written?"

They all smiled at the thought.

It had been a most interesting, and Sara and GiGi felt, successful afternoon. The company left about 4:30ish. Sara and GiGi began to clear away the glasses and dishes when Sara's phone rang. It was Sybil and she wanted to stop by for a few minutes. GiGi told Sara she'd leave and give her some time with her daughter but then she'd have to finish the cleaning up herself.

"Nonsense. Stay and see Sybil. We spend a lot of time alone so this can't be too important, just a casual drop by time. Perhaps she wants to find out how our little soiree went," Sara told GiGi.

"OK then I'll keep working." GiGi said, adding with a chuckle, "You just want me to stay for my excellent dish washing technique

— well actually, excellent dish towel work. They're your good glasses; you take care of the washing."

Sara agreed to that very quickly. After helping Sara, GiGi went home but that was not the end of the conversation.

"That was quite a revelation," Sara exclaimed on the phone later that night. "Wow, talk about romantic endings and interesting people too. All in all, I think a good time was had by all, don't you?"

"Absolutely. The Rabbi's statement was so appropriate too, since letters are always written on Yom Kippur," GiGi said. "Bet our Angels were having a great time saying 'See I told you so!' to any other Angels that would listen. No tugging at me either, how about you?"

"Nope. My Angels were having too good a time I think," said Sara.

"James was very quiet. So were David's wife Kristen and Rev. Emily," GiGi observed.

"Maybe he didn't want to take anything away from his parents' story. Seems like a nice enough young man and I think he approved of us as neighbors for his parents," Sara said.

"Where have you been keeping Emily? She certainly isn't one that's ready for retirement yet," GiGi inquired.

"Oh," Sara softly said, explaining, "She's the younger sister of one of my old high school chums. When I mentioned to my friend, Charlotte, who was coming to the party, she said 'I think my sister would fit right in there.' Turns out she is a Presbyterian minister who has just been waiting to come out of the closet. It's been a long time while her church decided to make the decision to accept openly gay people as ministers."

"Do you think she wanted to say anything about it?" GiGi asked. "She must have been pretty excited about the good news."

"I don't know and there was so much other stuff going on, don't think she had much of a chance. They all seemed to like each other and will probably be getting together again and then she can tell her story. Plus she's a lot younger than they are," Sara said.

"What does that have to do with it?" GiGi asked.

"I don't know, I just said it," Sara stated, "But it's true, in fact, there's Rev. Emily younger, Father Pat and Marie sort of semi-retired, and Rabbi Rappaport retired – three life stages – something like you, me and Ana."

"I hadn't thought of it that way. You're right and now it's time for another subject," GiGi said. "How is Sybil doing?"

"Well you remember that she still volunteers at the Jersey Battered Woman's Shelter, where she met her friend Debbie, you know, Robert's sister, a couple of years ago. They were both looking to help out and found a special friendship like we have," Sara said.

"Well of course. We know how volunteering can lead to all kinds of good things," GiGi stated. "In this case it led our Sybil to her Robert, and that seals it."

"Yes. So, she is very excited that her friend who was seeking help at the shelter has been able to get an apartment for herself and her two sons, and maybe even a job too. Now she has another friend who needs help and she's working on that one," Sara said.

GiGi smiled and thought to herself, "How funny it is that at first I was thinking Debbie was at the shelter because she needed protection. When all along she had her own life under control and was actually just helping others."

"What were you thinking?" asked Sara.

"Oh not much, just how sometimes one can get the wrong impression from some overheard words and not know the whole story," GiGi admitted.

"How true, I know I've done it, too" Sara said.

GiGi was glad to let the subject drop and asked, "Do you think we'll be invited to the next gathering of our new friends? Or we could do it again?"

"Of course," Sara declared. "They need the secular/humanist approach too."

"So that's what we are or at least something like that, but not always," GiGi said. "Look how we have Angels."

"Well I'm just confused," Sara confessed, with a sly smile.

"Yes, and that's for another night," GiGi chuckled.

And so it was.

CHAPTER 14

THE RABBI WANTS TO TELL A STORY

Sara called with the news that Rabbi Rappaport sent her a note asking her to come around and to bring her elder friend. "He meant you of course," she snickered. "Some elder friend, oh well, you are indeed a friend and my most special one too," she added.

"Well, you're no spring chicken yourself," GiGi smiled, pleased with herself, "What does he want with us old ladies?"

"It seems he's interested in your book. Can't imagine why," Sara teased.

"Probably because you've publicized it through the whole neighborhood, sometimes seems like the whole world," GiGi said. "I have people stopping me in the market asking how it's going. But let's get back to the Rabbi. I liked his quiet way. It should be interesting."

"Well, it's set for tomorrow afternoon, which is more convenient 2:30 or 4?" Sara asked.

"Well, 4 p.m. would be fine and then we can have dinner together to hash it all out —whatever we hear – not the dinner," GiGi joked.

"Funny," Sara said, "Stop by my apartment and we can go together."

"OK. See you tomorrow at 4. Oh, should I bring a tape recorder or take notes or – never mind, let's play it by ear," GiGi concluded. "It might be something real simple and not even worth putting in the book."

The plans were made and GiGi was pleased. The book was becoming very exciting – actually more challenging – and she hoped the Rabbi had a good story – as it would turn out he did. Well, actually his son did.

Now that the time was set to talk to the Rabbi, GiGi had another appointment she wanted to make with Sara. GiGi had received an invitation for a niece's wedding in four months. Naturally, she needed a new dress and wanted to call on Sara for guidance.

"Sara, I need help on shopping for a dress," GiGi said.

"You mean you're finally going to look more like 75 than 92 for a change – that's a switch for you. What's the occasion?" Sara joked.

"It's my niece, Honey, you know the skinny, sexy blond," GiGi explained.

"Oh yeah and which number is this one?" Sara asked with a chuckle.

"I think I stopped counting after two, but guess it's number five this time," GiGi said.

"And how many children does she have?" Sara asked. "Did you say six?"

"Now don't exaggerate," GiGi chided, "It's only four, all grown and on their own, thank goodness. I'm sure to hear all the gory details at the wedding."

"Oh I remember," Sara said, "She's the one you like so much."

"Yes, I'm very fond of her and the children," GiGi admitted. "It should be fun and now I need a special dress. How about meeting before the Rabbi and right after lunch – there are only a couple of shops I want to check out."

"Fine, how about 2 p.m. and that's plenty of time for the other appointment," Sara declared.

So time and place were arranged and GiGi felt pleased that she'd have a fashion guru, as she liked to call Sara, to help her.

When the next day arrived, the shop wasn't busy. Suddenly GiGi burst into the quiet of the salon laughing hysterically. Sara gave GiGi a quizzical look and asked "What on earth is happening with you?

Shopping is serious business and here you are giggling like a school girl. What gives?"

GiGi could hardly contain her laughter long enough to blurt out "All I can say is, it's a darn good thing I didn't buy another present."

Sara shook her head. She and the salesperson looked puzzled as she asked, "What the devil are you babbling about?"

GiGi's eyes twinkled as she revealed "You'll never guess who isn't getting married, as of this moment anyway."

Sara grinned with self-satisfaction as she guessed correctly "Honey, perhaps?"

GiGi replied "Sure, take away my fun of revealing it. You're too smart, Sara. Must be your psychic powers showing off again."

"So I'm right, as usual," Sara boasted.

"Of course you are Madame," GiGi said.

"So what happened between our phone plans and your dramatic entrance to alter our shopping mission?" Sara asked.

"Well, my daily snail mail arrived just as I was leaving to meet you. I opened a letter from Honey marked 'Important.' And there it is in big bold letters: **'IT'S OFF!! Not disappointed so don't worry about me. Talk soon, Love, Honey.'**"

"So now what do we do about dress shopping?" Sara said with a hint of disappointment.

"Well, I still need something to wear to your niece Molly's wedding," GiGi answered.

Noticing how empty the shop was, GiGi guessed it was the economy plus the time of day. Whatever, it made life easier for her. Sara wouldn't have minded – she always liked clothing challenges and having other customers milling around would not have bothered her a bit – not so for GiGi.

Besides shopping itself and the dress style, GiGi's challenge was color. "My favorites have always been blue and red and most of all the combination of white and black with sometimes a small dash of another color. I'm always aware of my bleached blond hair and fair complexion," she thought aloud, recalling, "I once was tested and they decided I was a 'winter' whatever that is."

Sara was having a great time talking with the salesperson. GiGi assumed they knew each other from their animated discussion. The two women decided to check out four different styles of dresses first. They could help GiGi decide on the color after. At this point, GiGi was relieved they were doing the initial choosing but knew that only she would make the final choice. "I still have some confidence in my ability to know what's right for me," GiGi thought. Then, when they brought out the dresses, GiGi had second thoughts, feeling they had to be kidding. But she took a deep breath and said to Sara, "OK, just for you, I'll try them on, but I don't really think they are my type."

"Well, at least you're willing to try – and willing to change your mind too – maybe?" Sara said hopefully.

The first one was not a go. The second had possibilities, the third one GiGi liked but Sara and the salesperson didn't. But the fourth was a knockout. It was definitely the one. GiGi couldn't believe it. It was so unappealing on the hanger, but really came alive when she tried it on.

"It looks great. Now for the color," said Sara asking GiGi, for the first time, what she wanted.

"I think blue," GiGi declared, adding "But a bright blue."

The salesperson checked the store and back room but found no blue dress.

"We have time, don't we?" GiGi asked Sara, "Molly's wedding isn't for a while, right?"

"That's true," Sara answered.

Turning to the salesperson, GiGi suggested "Try to get one and I'll – that is we'll – come back."

The salesperson said she would certainly do that. GiGi was pleased.

"It would be great to find just what I want and not have to do any more shopping," GiGi declared.

Sara agreed, and then when the two friends were outside the shop, she grabbed GiGi by the arm and started towards the other store around the corner.

"I thought we agreed to wait," GiGi protested.

"Uh-uh. We keep checking. At least we have one you really like. Anyhow, suppose the color doesn't seem right?" Sara said.

GiGi had to agree with the logic of shopping more, "just in case."

Just as they entered the next shop, GiGi took note of the time. "We need to hurry to our appointment," GiGi reminded Sara who had to agree with that logic, as well.

Happily for GiGi, shopping was finished for the day and she said, "Now let's head to the Rabbi's apartment for our next story."

"I'll buzz you right in, Ms. Bennington," came the cheerful announcement as Sara and GiGi waited at the elevator to take them to Rabbi Rappaport's apartment.

Startled, Sara said "I know that voice, how does he know who I am?"

The elevator doors opened and several small children came trooping out guided by two teenagers dressed in the latest low-slung khakis, no-sleeve undershirts and boots with untied laces trailing.

"Hi, Ms. Bennington," they shouted and headed towards the play area in the rear of the apartment building, herding the little ones out the back doors.

"You seem to be pretty popular today, Sara, from the deep tones to the screechy ones. Quite a selection I'd say," GiGi teased.

"The young ones I know, but that man's voice baffles me," Sara said.

"Well you won't have to think long because here we are," GiGi said as the elevator doors opened and they started down the hall and suddenly Sara said, "I bet I know who it is — want to bet me a cool coffee sundae next time we're celebrating my mysterious powers?"

"You're on," GiGi answered, not because she thought she would be right. But just because she was curious how Sara would get out of this one and GiGi told her so.

The apartment door opened and a tall, portly gentleman held the door open and smiled at Sara. "And how are you today," he asked and she replied, "Just fine, Jim, and I'm looking forward to a nice sundae one of these days. Let me give you a big hug."

"OK, enough of this," GiGi said. "How could you have known him from just that brief sentence on the intercom?"

Jim laughed and said, "Because that's how Ms. Bennington used to hear me. I was the cook at her school and loved to sing arias. The principal asked me to make all the announcements over the intercom. He knew the kids would listen to me and hope I'd sing some current song or two. I did hum a few bars every once in a while — just to keep the students on their toes."

By that time, Sara realized she needed to introduce GiGi and Jim. Then she said, "But what — how — why are you here at Rabbi Rappaport's?"

"It's a long story," Jim said as he ushered them into the living room, "I'll explain it after you visit with the Rabbi. He has a lot to tell you."

The room was a bit warm but the Rabbi still had a coverlet or two over his legs and he was his usual gracious, charming self, and laughing said, "I thought your reunion would be interesting. Glad it worked out but I've invited you here for another reason."

He waved at some deep cushiony chairs, the kind GiGi loved and always had trouble getting out of, and told the visitors to make themselves comfortable.

GiGi figured there were enough people to help get her up and sank into the chair.

"Mmm, hope I don't fall asleep," GiGi whispered to Sara and she nodded.

"Well, to begin," the Rabbi said turning to GiGi, "You are writing that book about bullying and also about letters people write to heal relationships, right?"

GiGi assured him she was, and that she always looked for interesting stories.

The Rabbi explained, "It's actually my son David's story and he planned to be here and then his secretary called and said that an important client needed to see him. He had to leave but gave me permission to tell you his story and he could always add to it later.

"Being reformed, not Orthodox Jews, my wife, Naomi, and I did not keep a Kosher home and were fairly lenient in our attitude about other religions and people. Our children, David in particular, seldom even came to the synagogue. This distressed my wife a lot but I told her we would not force anything on them. They would find out their own beliefs for themselves and eventually they did," the Rabbi explained.

"David went off to college – a somewhat liberal one – that he had worked hard to get into. Then he paid off his college loans and finally received his MBA. When he returned home all he could talk about was this special girl who lived only two towns away from us. He had met her at college and they were sort of semi-engaged and he wanted us to meet her. Naomi wanted to know if she was Jewish and he said no but it didn't matter to either of them. She didn't go to her church and felt pretty much the way he did about religion," the Rabbi continued.

"Then Naomi asked how her family felt about this relationship. David sort of avoided this question and said that he hadn't met them yet. 'Oh, you're sort of engaged but neither family knows either of you, David?' Then I asked, 'When did you plan on letting us meet your friend and what's her name, please?' David flushed and said, 'Sorry I meant to say that right away. It's Colleen Murphy and she has red hair as well.' We all laughed. That was the only laughter for that day. This was really very serious business and Naomi and I weren't sure what we could expect next," the Rabbi recalled.

Then, as if on schedule, came the little ones the women had seen coming out of the elevator a while before and their shepherds – a bit tired from the way they dragged their boots. But the little ones just jumped on the Rabbi and tried to tell him what had happened.

Well it was obvious that David's story would have to wait for another time – and GiGi and Sara motioned to Jim that this was a good time to leave. They wanted to hear his story and told the Rabbi. He agreed quickly, as the children hugged and kissed him.

"Story, story Rabbi, tell us a story and then we'll tell you ours," the little ones said and they settled around him on the huge sofa. This seemed to be a normal happening and it was sweet to watch.

Jim helped GiGi out of that deep chair and they went out into the hall where there were some benches and he told his story, beginning with, "When last you saw me, Ms. Bennington..."

"Please call me Sara," she interjected.

"OK, Sara. Well, I was the cook at your school when my wife became quite ill. I took time off to care for her. But I had to resign. It became obvious she would need me for a very long time. I learned a lot about nursing, I can tell you, and luckily she wasn't in too much pain. This went on for two years and then she had a massive stroke and died.

I took time to visit relatives here and there across the states and even in Europe and tried to plan my next step," Jim explained.

"On my way home," Jim continued, "Thinking of going back to cooking or baking, I suddenly realized I didn't much care for that anymore – the hot kitchen, crowded space, constant preparation and then constant cleaning up. It just wasn't appealing. Instead I decided to give nursing a try. So I applied at a home health care agency, and well, here I am. But this is a different kind of nursing; I am more of a companion. In fact I live here and have certain hours and days off. It has worked out very well for all of us, Rabbi's family and even those dear little ones – active all the time – I love it, especially because I miss my own grandchildren."

Sara chuckled and said she understood how lucky he, the Rabbi and the children were to have this special relationship.

Just then GiGi looked at her watch and said, "Sara, we need to get going."

Sara turned to Jim and said, "Please tell the Rabbi we will be in touch."

Then GiGi and Sara went on their way. They definitely had much to hash over.

Sara and GiGi talked briefly by phone that night. "I wonder," Sara said, "If David was really away on business."

"Those were my thoughts as well. Do you think it was too painful to tell – but if so, why did he have his father call us over to tell the story?" GiGi asked.

"Yeah, we only met David briefly a couple of times. What did you think of him?" Sara inquired.

"Sort of laid back – not someone with a lot of mystery about him," GiGi replied.

"Well it's certainly a mystery as to why he called on us, that's for sure," Sara stated, adding, "There we go again – judging and there could be a fantastic story for your book."

"What I wonder is, if there will ever be a story," GiGi said. "You know – it's happened before. People start to tell some secret and then it's too painful or whatever and they don't finish."

Sara said, "Well maybe they will at least write a letter – remember how it helped me."

"Yes, and how it's helped me too – guess the Angels are hugging each other. And now it seems a good time to wish you pleasant dreams and good night," GiGi said.

"You too," said Sara, and then added almost under her breath, "I hope David can sleep well too."

GiGi added to herself, "I doubt it," and still to herself, "For some reason, don't know why I just felt that David wasn't ready yet. Maybe the Angels tugged at me, whatever."

In any case, there was the Father Pat story that needed to be followed up – and then GiGi wondered what Sara was thinking and hoped she would have a good night's sleep.

The next day the phone rang. This time Father Pat called GiGi first – she explained that she needed Sara for her "ears" and asked if he minded.

"Of course not and let's set a tentative date," he responded.

"OK let's do that," GiGi agreed and they proceeded to make their arrangements for a time convenient for all. They set it for Thursday.

When GiGi called Sara with the time and date to meet with Father Pat, they chatted about him and wondered, of course, what was his reason for telling his story?

"Maybe he was involved somehow in something mysterious," Sara speculated.

"Nope. Can't picture that," GiGi said and Sara agreed.

"True, but then why?" Sara asked. The two continued wondering, guessing and surmising,

"It's probably something very simple – a really good reason without all the questions we've raised," Sara finally said. "In any case we'll know on Thursday."

"True – but we always seem to like trying to guess ahead of time, don't we?" GiGi asked.

"Yeah, it's a challenge, I guess." Sara said, "To see if we're right."

Sometimes they were. But they would have to wait to find out if they were this time. They said their goodbyes and hung up for the night.

It would not be too long before the dress shop salesperson called, a few days after the first shopping trip there. The news in that day's call was that GiGi's blue dress had come in. "When did you want to see it?" the saleswoman asked.

"I'll have to call you back," GiGi replied.

Shortly after that, GiGi called Sara to tell her that the dress was in. GiGi called the salesperson and arranged to go the next day to see the dress.

The next afternoon, when GiGi tried it on, she was still pleased with the dress and arranged for a fitting.

The color was just right. Now she needed the necessities like shoes, purse, etc. She decided to ask Sara for more help. She could pick out those items—but she did need a ride to the shops. Sara was always more than willing to drive her any place. But GiGi still resented having to ask people for rides. Many times they offered but losing this last independence (as she thought of it) always bothered her. "I know," she said aloud to herself to make an even stronger point. "I am so lucky to have all these friends—they're my earthly Angels."

GiGi mused, "I wonder if they realize how important they are to me and each other. Yeah, I think they do. When one of us has a problem—it seems everyone gathers round and somehow it may be pretty bad but not as terrible as it could be without our Angels."

GiGi remembered how she had been an earthly Angel to many people over these past 92 years. "Well," she said to herself, "I really can't count more than 70 of those years, when I was a bit older. It seems what goes around always comes around, as it's said."

It helped to remind herself that she too had helped many others along the way. She was not bragging, just remembering. Then she thought if more people remembered that, it might make it easier for them to accept help themselves and to remember that the ones who are helping now, will eventually need help themselves too.

GiGi smiled to herself and thought, "You've managed to cheer yourself up again."

And so it was.

CHAPTER 15

GIGI HAS A DREAM

A couple of days after their talking about David and Father Pat sharing their stories, Sara and GiGi were following up a lead about Leila and little Daniel. It brought them to an office building in the city.

As they stood on the elevator, there was an air of disappointment palpable between them even as they were jostled by other riders being swallowed up or disgorged from the elevator as it made its way down to the lobby.

"Well, I guess David Rappaport does want to tell his story," Sara muttered, almost under her breath.

GiGi stared at her with a puzzled expression and asked "What brought that on?'

"Shhh, we're in the elevator and I can't explain now. Later," Sara said.

Finally, they were able to get off and make their way outside the office building, where the search had turned out to be just another dead end.

"Let's stop at this coffee shop and I'll explain everything," Sara said.

"OK," GiGi agreed, "And it will help to have some tea to wash away the disappointment of another dead end about your Daniel and Leila, I guess."

"Yes, maybe that might help," Sara said unconvincingly.

They got their drinks and sat down. GiGi looking a bit impatient said, "OK spill it. How did you know David wants to talk?"

"Well as it turns out, while you were in the ladies' room at the lawyer's office earlier, I got a cell phone call from David. But because there were so many people around I just didn't have any opportunity to bring you up to date, that's all," Sara explained.

Sara added that David had suggested they come to his father's apartment so he could finish the story his father started. Sara asked GiGi when she wanted to go. GiGi thought Friday would be good – sometime after lunch.

Sara called David on her cell phone and the appointment was made.

GiGi and Sara finished running their other errands for the day and went home.

That night GiGi had a dream about the book. It wasn't upsetting or even scary. It was just the sort of dream that helped to spell out things – to make life clearer. So she decided to share it with Sara when next they met.

Sitting on their favorite park bench they seemed to be sort of set off – apart from any other activities that usually went on around, over and all about them.

It was almost like a sacred place – at least in GiGi's mind – and then Sara said "Did you notice how quiet this space is?"

GiGi said, "I did and it sets just the right feeling to describe my dream."

"You sound kind of spooky," Sara said.

"No, not at all just something special to me," and GiGi started to describe her dream.

"Sara, you are more aware than most other people how important this book is to me."

"Of course, and I share your feelings, but I guess not as strongly. There is so much else going on in my life," Sara admitted.

"I know and that's why it's so important to know how you would feel after hearing my dream," GiGi stated.

"Well, I won't know what to say until I hear the dream you're working up to telling. It gives me a little shiver," and then Sara did actually shiver.

"I'm sorry," GiGi said. "I don't mean to frighten you. My dream is really all about good stuff and the book, if you agree it's doable. OK, OK here it is."

"Sorry, I was just carried away thinking how alike we are in so many ways," Sara said.

"Yes we are. Anyhow, last night, I suddenly woke up. Guess my Angels started tugging at me pretty hard and I realized, 'Hey I'm 92 and writing an important book, at least to me. What happens if I die and there it sits, never getting published, never helping people heal?'" GiGi confessed.

"Why do you have to think of dying?" Sara asked, seeming a bit annoyed. "You are in great health. No big problems aside from a fall. Now you are being spooky and I don't like this conversation."

"Sara, please listen to the rest of it. I have thought about dying before. How can I not? I have always hoped it would be either in my sleep or in a quiet way like my mother and just peacefully go off. After all, she was 93 and my dad 96 when they died," GiGi said.

"But you always said you wanted to live to 100," Sara declared.

"Well, of course I still feel that way, assuming quality of life is still good. But this isn't about me as much as the book," GiGi stated.

"How can the book matter at that point?" Sara scoffed.

"But it does and this is my question for you. If the book isn't finished when I die, would you be willing to finish it and get it published?" GiGi implored.

"How could I possibly do that? I can't write like you or certainly as well. People would know right away it wasn't you. After all you'll be dead at that point. Ugh, what an awful thought," Sara said shaking her head.

"I know. I have thought of that. There would be papers I left for you to finish the book," GiGi assured Sara.

"You seem to have thought a lot about this. But how could I finish it? It sounds crazy," Sara said.

"No, it isn't. Remember how our Angels have helped us with their tugging and their thoughts or whatever Angels have. They were conveyed to us somehow and voila things were done," GiGi said confidently.

"Yeah, things were done. You make it sound so simple and anyhow, Angels don't write books, or do they?" Sara teased.

"That's my plan. I'll be there, sort of near you and suggesting what should be written, sort of like your Archangel," GiGi stated confidently.

"Sure," Sara interrupted, "That's your plan. What guarantee is there?"

"There isn't any of course. All I can do is ask you to trust me and the book and at least agree to take it on. I believe we are so much alike that you will feel me near. Then if I don't appear, well, that's the end and no book," GiGi said in a way of releasing Sara from the obligation.

"I must be out of my mind to even think of it. Number one to think of you dead isn't doable. Number two, my trying to write this book is also not doable," Sara said emphatically.

"Sara, I promise to try to stay alive till 100. But in the meantime, could we at least think this could work and I'll feel a lot better about the book?" GiGi implored again.

"Yeah, yeah, lay on the guilt," Sara replied.

Suddenly the air, the whole atmosphere around them seemed livelier with a lot of activity. It felt like a good sign to GiGi that Sara would agree. But she didn't want to press any more. She knew Sara had enough to think about at this point. And then…

"OK, crazy as it seems, I'll think – just think – about it," Sara agreed and smiling added, "Now let's go get our favorite ice cream. I want a cone this time. It's more earthly."

They enjoyed their yummy ice cream cones before parting for the day.

The next morning GiGi remembered Sara's call saying she had a report, as she called it. She had met Pat or Father Pat as he was called, in the elevator and he asked again about the book. Was GiGi really serious about all the different kinds of bullying that people encounter and writing about it? Sara said, "I assured him that you were very serious and that it was important that people become aware of it and how to handle the problem."

GiGi said, "Thanks Sara, I would like to find out what his story might be. How do I get in touch with him?" GiGi was excited about the opportunity and wanted to get started.

Sara reminded her, "You met him at the wine and cheese party I had, why don't you look up his number and call?"

GiGi thought it was a good idea and she'd start right away and hung up. Then she called back quickly to thank her for the lead and followed up with her usual question for Sara of "How do you meet so many interesting people willing to share their stories?"

Sara's usual reply followed. "It's that special touch," and they both laughed – and hung up.

Later, GiGi's Angels tugged at her again and she remembered that it was time for the appointment with Father Pat. GiGi had invited them to her place thinking he would probably be amused by all the funny, silly and beautiful Angels she had accumulated over the years and he was.

GiGi was sitting in her apartment with Father Pat and "her ears" as she often referred to Sara.

Father Pat was admiring GiGi's many Angels, and before long he was telling stories of some of his own earthly Angels.

Father Pat began to tell his story by saying he had been approached by a young man in his parish school that he was going to call Tommy. Father Pat said it was not the boy's real name. Anyway he said this Tommy came to him to tell him about a letter he had gotten from another boy in the school.

Suddenly Father Pat's cell phone rang – it was Marie saying that a parishioner named Mrs. Frazier was dying and her family wanted him to hurry to the hospital – the whole family was there. Father Pat rose quickly and said, "I'm so sorry but we'll have to continue another time," and he quickly left.

Since the Father Pat story had to be delayed, Sara decided to take her ears and leave as well. And so it was.

CHAPTER 16

DAVID STARTS HIS EMOTIONAL STORY

T he day of their next appointment with David, Jim ushered them into what seemed to be a private study in Rabbi Rappaport's apartment. It must have been chosen for privacy. The beautiful wooden bookcases were filled with books of all sizes and colors, with bright and dull leather bindings. It had some order up to a point and then the books seemed to just overflow tables, the floor, even some chairs. David apologized as he moved books off chairs. He explained it was his pleasure to bring order to this, but he had been too busy. He obviously loved books. He motioned the two women to be seated in the chairs he had uncovered and sat in a chair in front of the desk. He was dressed casually in Dockers and a colorful blue and green Rugby shirt.

David began, "Sorry we couldn't finish this before but at least we can do it now. I understand my father had to stop when he was explaining my relationship with Colleen and how I told it to my parents. Let me pick up where he left off. My mother was very unhappy, my dad not as much."

David continued, "Dad was just concerned that we might be too hasty and not take enough time to get to know each other and our families. In any case, Colleen and I decided that our love was enough and that family objections could be smoothed over. We went off to Vegas and were married. Ah, youth and youthful love. Colleen's parents were as appalled as my mother had been and asked to meet with my parents. They wanted us to have an annulment. After many planned meetings that never took place, we all eventually met."

David shifted around in his chair as he spoke, continuing, "Colleen and I were adamant. Colleen was pregnant. We were thrilled and were certain that our families would come around once they knew about the baby. And they did."

He paused briefly then continued. "After some time we managed to adjust to having a newborn and our lives seemed to be regaining some normalcy. But then when I approached Colleen she always had a headache. At other times it was 'too soon.' She always had an excuse. She had never reacted that way before – in fact she had initiated sex as often as I had. I had read how women could react differently because of hormonal changes so after several months I suggested we see a specialist. Our sex life before the baby had always been frequent and satisfying for both of us. She refused at first but eventually agreed to see someone alone."

At this point, David asked if Sara and GiGi would like some tea. He confessed he would like a short break too. Sara and GiGi agreed it was a good idea. He called Jim and asked if he would bring them some refreshments.

Almost immediately Jim entered with different teas and some yummy looking biscuits. It seemed to relieve some of the tension in the room as they busily picked a special tea over others. As they sipped, David explained he had spent a lot of time in England. He discovered that tea time always helped when relaxation was needed – and he needed it now. Sara and GiGi agreed – they needed it too.

After a few minutes David started his story again. "Colleen went to her doctor who suggested she see a therapist. She made several appointments but would never tell me anything about their talks. I didn't expect her to. But her frigidity continued and she didn't seem to want to change. After about six months of therapy, she asked if I would like to accompany her to the next session. It was arranged for the following week."

David continued, "I was a bit apprehensive about the meeting but it was nothing compared to Colleen's anxiety. During the next days she kept saying she wondered if this was a good idea. I never responded fearing she would change the plan. Well, when we finally arrived at the therapist's home office, we were both pretty nervous. The waiting room was furnished with comfortable chairs and soft lighting. It was meant for reassurance and I felt so. Even Colleen seemed to relax a bit. We waited only a few minutes and then were ushered into the doctor's office. The therapist was young and attractive. Colleen introduced us and then explained that she was not able to tell me her problem. However, she had asked her doctor to tell me. It seemed strange but I was glad to be able to hear whatever it was from someone."

David poured another cup of tea and held it tenderly. He needed a couple of moments to continue.

"When we were seated on the couch, Dr. Rita Jameson turned to me and began with: "David, Colleen never meant for this to happen and I must tell you that Colleen and I have been working together for the past several months. As her therapist, we have worked very intensively to help her understand her decision to ask for a divorce."

David stared off into the distance not looking at either Sara or GiGi as he continued, "I don't know if I was in shock or what because all I could do at that moment was sit silently staring at the two of them. I found myself clenching and relaxing my fists over and over again. I think I felt the need to break something but there was nothing for me to break. Maybe it was my heart that was being broken at that moment. I just know that those words were the last thing I was expecting."

GiGi started to say "David, I wonder…" when there was sudden knocking on the door.

Jim called out, "David, Kristy needs you." David rose suddenly and said, "That's my daughter. I'd better check to see what's happening. Please excuse me." And he walked quickly to the door.

Sara and GiGi said they would call later. The story, as they hastened from the library, still surrounded them.

Sara suggested going for tea and GiGi said "Oh yes, please—right away." They walked slowly, turned a street corner and noticed a small shop with signs in the window announcing tea and coffee. It looked cozy and they hurried in. They obviously needed to relax after David's story and some personal memories of their own. When they were seated, and had been served their tea, Sara asked GiGi what she thought.

GiGi said, "I'm not sure this should be in the book. It's so personal, I don't know."

Sara said, "There must be more, he mentioned Kristy, there must be more, maybe lots more."

"Well, we'll see. David's too busy with his daughter now. Let's wait to find out how she is. I hope it's not serious." GiGi continued, "I wonder how old she is. I wonder a lot of things, don't you?"

Sara nodded.

"David sounds like he was stunned by the news" said GiGi, "But he seems to be doing OK now, don't you think? I wonder how he's reached his present life, or if he really is OK."

"Well, we'll have to wonder until he's able to finish his story. Oh by the way, remember we have an appointment with Father Pat tomorrow," Sara reminded GiGi. "It's time to switch gears and get ready for the next story."

GiGi said with a sigh, "Will do."

Later that evening, Sara called. "Your 'ears' are hereby reporting that David said Kristy just scraped her knee and was now fine. Little 5 year old girls need lots of loving when they have accidents, as he put it. She added, "If you're able and willing we have another appointment for Saturday."

GiGi was glad to hear that Kristy was OK and about the appointment. "Maybe," she thought, "We'll finally hear why he thinks it will be good for the book and hear the rest of his story."

The Angels tugged at her to remind her to switch gears for the appointment with Father Pat.

"Thanks, Angels, it has been quite an emotional day and I am sleepy," GiGi said out loud to herself, and them, as she settled under her comfy bed covers and was asleep almost as soon as her head touched the pillow.

It was the next day when Sara and GiGi met with Father Pat. This time the meeting was in Father Pat's and Marie's apartment.

As they entered the family room GiGi felt right at home. It had a couple of New England rocking chairs, divided by a modern table with a small fish tank.

"Another 'fishamologist,'" GiGi thought, "Just like Sara. Guess she'll feel right at home."

There were lots of pillows that ranged from deep purple to the delft blue that dominated the room. So many curios and vases, filled with flowers, and everything seemed to meld together. There were wonderfully comfortable soft chairs, just deep enough to make you cozy but not too much, so GiGi could get up easily. She loved the bright blues and softer lavenders. The pictures were special too. They were old maps of all different colors and shapes and books that crowded each other for attention with their bright dust covers. All in all, the ambiance, as GiGi always loved to say, was just wonderful. She noticed Sara glancing around too. They would surely have a ball later talking about what they liked the most.

Marie offered them something to drink and snack on. GiGi chose lemonade and biscuits and settled on a rocking chair. She asked if she could put her drink on the marble table and was assured that it could do no harm. This is her kind of home, GiGi thought, relaxed and welcoming.

Father Pat came into the room. As usual, he had been on his cell phone. He sat on the other rocking chair and took out a pipe. Sara and GiGi looked at each other, but said nothing. He seemed to feel it necessary to explain: "Marie allows me one pipeful a week. Then she is always busy putting out candles to take away the odor."

As if on call, at that moment Marie was placing candles all around the room. She asked GiGi and Sara "Would pipe smoke be OK?"

"I can answer for myself," GiGi said, "It's OK. Then Sara added her OK too.

There definitely would be lots more to talk about later, GiGi thought.

Marie seemed to feel a need to explain, saying, "He used to smoke at least 6 to 8 or more hours a day, so we compromised on this 'once in a while'."

"So far it's worked," Father Pat said, "Thanks to my thoughtful wife. I'm grateful for that and my improved health as well. But enough about my little foible, if I can call it that. Let's continue about Tommy, which is not his real name of course. I hope you remember where we left off."

GiGi said she did. "I remember you telling the story of Tommy coming to you with a letter another boy had written him. But then, your cell phone rang and you had an emergency that needed attention. You suggested continuing another time—and here we are."

"Well here it is," replied Father Pat. With that, he unfolded the white, blue lined school paper page, ink blots and all.

"*Tommy,*" he read in a low, serious voice, "*After last week when you pushed me in the steel fence, teacher sent me to the nurse when she saw the big gash on my leg. I told her I fell playing ball but she didn't believe me. I didn't want to but she finally found out what happened.*

Now I have to write a letter to you and one to Father Pat. She is going to check them over.

I didn't want to write but here it is——she made me and said things would be better.

Anyways, she wants me to tell you that I want to be friends and not be hit on all the time.

And to tell you I wear glasses or I can't see right and I have trouble with my hip.

Tony."

After a few moments, the silence was broken by Sara saying how brave Tony was. Father Pat agreed and added "that he had the school nurse to thank for encouraging him and sending him to me." He smiled as he said this and continued. "Remember your wine and cheese soiree and your kindness in including our son James, well there's more to the story. He felt comfortable after meeting you and discovering plans for your book, GiGi. He said it was OK to share his story."

GiGi and Sara looked curiously at what Father Pat had just said, as he continued with his story.

"Now to get back to what followed after Tony's letter. Tommy and I had a long talk and he confessed he picked on Tony only because all the other kids did. He actually had liked Tony when he first came to school. After our talk, he befriended Tony and there was no more bullying. But what did follow was my interest in him. I knew his widowed mother was raising him on her own even though she was in poor health. They were alone, no relatives. Well, I think you guessed the rest of the story. Yes, James was Tommy and we were able to adopt him several years ago when his mother died. GiGi and Sara, I think your angels were working overtime for us."

Marie suggested they all relax and maybe this time have some sherry. That sounded good all-around and they chatted for a few more minutes, admired the fish, flowers and the wonderful smelling candles – the pipe had long gone out – and then Sara and GiGi said their goodbyes and promised to meet again soon. It was so good, GiGi thought, to really mean it with these warm people and she suspected they felt the same, or at least she hoped so. She and Sara had much to discuss once more.

CHAPTER 17

ANOTHER STORY FOR
THE BOOK

The days seemed to be consumed with meeting about stories for the book. Sara was excited about a planned meeting she and GiGi had with a more contemporary person to GiGi's age. As Sara had said, with a twinkle, "Let's hear her memories of your old days."

Sara explained to GiGi, Anita had recently moved to the area and knew no one. She had been a best friend to Sara's Aunt Jane years ago. Sara admitted she had played liaison several states away and to her family, resulting, she bragged, in this present appointment. Anita knew the purpose of GiGi's book and was thinking she might be able to contribute a story.

GiGi was also excited, but a bit more subdued than Sara. GiGi knew how Sara sometimes moved too quickly. She hoped this one would be as good as she bragged about. In any case, they were about to find out, since Anita was expected at Sara's in just a few minutes.

Anita, not familiar with the neighborhood, was hoping she had allowed enough time to be on time. She had met Sara many times when she visited Jane and was looking forward to meeting GiGi. Anita had talked to Sara about GiGi saying, "She sure sounds interesting, writing about bullying and letters that help heal, at her age. Sounds like some kind of inspiration. I certainly could write some stories on my own. Well, maybe. I want to relax and enjoy checking out the city again."

Anita had apparently given the whole move a lot of thought.

"Maybe my story could help," Anita had told Sara. "I've been advocating writing letters, even when not sent, for years. That's what we social workers had always done."

Well before long there she was at the building where the apartment was. Anita pressed the button just on time. She was greeted by Sara who invited her into a lovely, comfortably furnished family room. GiGi, already seated next to a walker, enthusiastically greeted her.

Anita was a pleasant looking woman of medium build who liked dressing in brightly colored clothing. It was something she started doing at some point as a way of asserting herself in the world. GiGi liked the way she looked in the bright colors with an air of confidence about her. GiGi thought Anita looked like someone she and Sara would enjoy having as a friend.

"Welcome to our town. Please forgive my not rising," GiGi said. "My back is not cooperating today."

From her greeting and smile, Anita immediately felt at home. Sara motioned for her to sit in one of the comfortable looking chairs and they all settled in.

"We hope you'll enjoy our little town as much as we do," GiGi continued, "but I suspect Sara has already given you the rah-rah routine." They all smiled and Sara, leading right to the subject at hand, added, "Yeah and about the book too."

Anita laughed and said, "OK, let's get started." She decided the best place to start would be the beginning.

"My background is liberal, cultural Jewish, agnostic, on a spiritual journey. We lived in New York City and belonged to many progressive organizations and enjoyed the city's many art offerings. I worked part-time for a union while going to night school and kept busy with several boyfriends as well. At 20, I still had not found the right one," Anita stated.

"Oh, have to digress for a moment to mention one of the most terrible moments in my life. There was a union rally at Union Square that year that was attended by police on horseback. I don't know why, I just happened to stop at the rally and was absolutely terrified by those horses. The rally was relatively quiet, well organized, so I never understood why the horses were necessary. In any case, I understand and sympathize with how participants at some of these recent events in the Occupy Wall Street Movement must have felt," Anita said, with a hint of trepidation in her voice, then adding, "Sorry, I didn't mean to stray so far from my planned story."

Sara thanked her for the side-track and said she quite understood how Anita felt. "It must have been very frightening," Sara said quietly. "Actually, I had planned to have tea shortly. Maybe now is a good time. OK with you two?"

Anita and GiGi agreed and chatted with each other as if they had been years' long friends.

After their tea and yummy biscuits, Anita said she was ready to continue her story.

"It started when Alan and I met and after that, there was no one else for me. We felt the same politically, enjoyed the same books, music and art. I felt I'd met my soul mate and he seemed to feel the same. My parents were very fond of him and they had many animated political discussions. He was also working and going to school at night but we managed to spend a lot of time together.

"As I look back now, it seems strange that we never had sex—just the usual hugging and kissing but no sleeping together. Some of my other boyfriends had been mostly interested in having sex even though there were few places we could go. This was definitely not the same kind of relationship and I deeply regret that now. But I won't digress this time except to make note of how naive I, well, all of us, were."

Anita continued, "It really was a pretty day for March 1st. Alan, my mother and I – my dad had to work – went to the municipal courthouse and we were married. When we got home, I think we went out to celebrate. I'm hazy on that. I don't remember too much except that for me it was all a dream come true, marrying Alan and also, another big one, finally leaving home."

"Were you pregnant and had to get married?" asked GiGi, following Anita's suggestion to ask questions to help her remember details of over 60 years ago. Anita chuckled and said, "Remember I told you we never had sex."

"Oh that's right, I forgot," GiGi said.

Anita continued, "Several weeks later, Alan was sitting in the park with his two older sisters and their husbands and suddenly Hank, Rose's husband, said to Alan 'You seem to be worried like an old married man.' It was then Alan told them 'I am.' As Alan told me later, there were all kinds of probing questions from his sisters – who, what, where, why, and so on. As I think back now, how could their darling younger brother have done such a thing without them involved, was probably at the top of his sisters' list. Little did they know that would have been the last thing he wanted. He wanted to leave his home same as I did. Probably those desires took precedence over any other feelings."

"Did you know them at all?" asked Sara.

"No, I never met his family, not even until April 24, the official wedding day," Anita replied.

"Alan told me how his mother threatened to commit suicide and his father was ready to send him off to an expensive out of state college. Alan was working and going to NYU night school, for which his parents were helping to pay. I will say that his sisters were finally able to get his mother to agree to come to the wedding but his father still refused because I was Jewish."

GiGi interjected. "It was a done deal. There wasn't much they could do, was there?"

Anita nodded and then continued. "So, we rented a studio apartment on 33rd Street right off 3rd Avenue. It was necessary to do this because remember in those days, prior to 1983, Catholics had to publish the names of those getting married, usually in their local parish news. It was called publishing the 'banns.' But in our case it was decided it should be done outside the Bronx where we all lived. Manhattan was determined to be the 'safest' place, and then no one except Alan's family would know who I was."

"How did your family feel about all this," murmured GiGi. "Were they upset or what?"

"Actually I don't think I told them about all this. Nor did I tell them about my going to St. Patrick's Cathedral to be instructed by a priest on how to bring up our future children. Since they, Alan and I were all non-believers, guess they would have thought it the right thing just to make Alan's mother happy," Anita said.

"Did you ever wonder about your parents not suggesting meeting Alan's family, or not getting married so hastily or something? Did they think you were pregnant?" asked GiGi.

"That was probably on everyone's mind," Anita admitted, "But it was never mentioned. Those were the days when you didn't talk openly about that."

"But you lived through all that and then came the second wedding day? Was it better now that the other stuff was over and you were at least going to meet the family?" GiGi asked.

"Well, all except Alan's father. Not until several years later, probably when he had a grandchild. I don't remember that special occasion. Suddenly he was just there at family gatherings when he hadn't been before. I don't think anyone really cared. No, I take that back. The sisters cared because they had talked him into buying a car. He didn't drive and they could borrow it whenever they wanted."

"Did he mind?" asked GiGi.

"I don't think so because he didn't even have a driver's license and liked being driven around with the family," Anita replied.

"Is this important?" asked Sara "Who cares that they borrowed the car, etc.?"

"Well, as it turns out it was very important because the girls, a.k.a. the sisters, arranged for us to have the car for April 24th, our big wedding day," Anita recalled, appearing a little sad as she was dredging up all these memories.

GiGi, sensing Anita could use a little break, said quietly, "How about some more tea and those delicious biscuits, Sara?"

"Sounds good to me," said Anita.

Sara obviously thought so too as she left the room to get them.

After a few minutes of sipping the relaxing tea, Anita said she was ready to continue the story. "We, meaning my parents, Alan's mother, his two sisters and their husbands, the priest and Alan and me, of course, were waiting in the Our Lady Chapel of St. Patrick's Cathedral. We were waiting for my cousin who was supposed to be my matron of honor. She was late and I was getting a bit more nervous wondering what to do. All I know is that one of the sisters became my matron of honor. Don't even remember which one. We didn't find out until days later that my cousin, who was a religious Jew, approached the door to Our Lady Chapel and couldn't enter, She said she just froze, couldn't find anyone to tell them to notify me and she left."

"Wow, that must have been terrible for you," said GiGi.

"I guess so, but I don't remember anything of the ceremony or anything else until after my parents took us all out to a lovely little French restaurant to celebrate. Then everyone took their various routes to respective homes. Alan and I took the car to do some shopping. I remember we went to Altman's and picked out glassware and china retrieved the silver service we had ordered and started home to our 3rd Avenue and 33rd Street studio."

Sara exclaimed "What a strain for you and Alan, well actually for everyone, now that I think of it. Bet you all were glad it was over without anything else bad happening."

"Welllll," Anita said.

"Uh oh," GiGi exclaimed. "What? What happened?"

"The 3rd Avenue trolley tracks happened," Anita continued. "We skidded and damaged his father's car. Alan and I just had slight head bumps but we were pretty badly shaken up. As I look back now, Alan probably had too much to drink and we were lucky the police didn't cite him for it. Guess they felt sorry for us since it was our wedding day. Had to call my parents to ask for help since the garage mechanic said it would cost $100 and we didn't have that much available just like that."

"Your parents must have been very upset and worried," GiGi said.

"Yes," Anita said, "They were and insisted that we come to their house so they could see how we really were. When they checked us over, they were satisfied we had just a few bruises. My dad gave us the money and we were off to our new home. As I think back now, he probably paid some loan shark to get us the money but Alan and I never even though of that at the time. We were just grateful, exhausted and anxious to get home. What a day it had been!!"

"Did you have any kind of honeymoon or what?" GiGi asked.

"We had planned to take off a few days of work and just enjoy visiting museums and maybe a show or two. Money was tight and would be even tighter now with the car repairs to be made. Plus we had to keep the accident a secret from his family," Anita said. "Yes, I know, you want to know what happened on our first night. Well, nothing and nothing continued to happen for the next three years."

"Didn't you guys love each other? What was wrong?" GiGi asked. "Well, it's certainly understandable on your wedding night after all that disaster."

"Yes, I thought the same thing," Anita recalled. "After many months, I finally went for therapy since I couldn't talk with Alan about the problem. He always started to drink his sherry the minute he was home and after he consumed it for hours, was in bed, asleep and snoring very quickly."

"What did the therapist say?" GiGi asked.

"Well, he wanted Alan to come in with me but I couldn't even mention this to Alan, it was too embarrassing," recalled Anita, looking a bit embarrassed even all these years later.

Sara and GiGi tried not to glance at each other. Their thoughts practically collided and exploded in mid-air. The air certainly was heavy with theirs and Anita's emotions as she continued.

"It had reached the point, for me, that I thought he didn't love me, was sorry he had even married me and on and on. I wasn't good enough for him. You name it and I thought it," Anita admitted.

"Oh how awful," Sara said. "And you had no one to talk to?"

"That was the other part. No sisters or anyone I felt I could tell about this awful thing. It must be all my fault. What could I do, so I just lived on," Anita said.

"How did the other stuff work out with you not being Catholic?" GiGi asked.

"That's another story and don't feel like going into that now," Anita confessed. "Think you can wait for that next chapter another day?"

"Of course," GiGi agreed. "You've done enough past living for now and we can both remind you that you have come a long way, baby and you deserve applause for it."

GiGi rose slowly from her chair, and walked over to Anita to give her a big hug and kiss. With many tears, she thanked Anita for being willing to share, and even to continue her story. GiGi said she would be honored if Anita would allow her story to be included in the book.

And so it was.

During the next morning's usual phone call GiGi said to Sara, "How about that story last night? My Angels knew Anita needed some time to continue the story after the wedding. How about your Angels?"

"You read their minds as usual. I was already thinking of inviting Anita back for a meal to give her a chance to tell us the rest of her story. What do you think of that?" Sara said, with a chuckle.

"Of course, it makes all the sense in the world or should we say the other world? Ha ha," GiGi retorted.

Sara called Anita to ask if tomorrow night was good for her. Anita had responded to Sara's invitation with: "That would be great. Take me away from all these boxes that need to be unpacked and remind me how lucky I am to be here—not back 40 years ago."

Naturally, Sara shared Anita's response with GiGi.

GiGi thought how lucky she was too. Living now, despite some health inconveniences, was one of the best times of her life. It always amazed her when she told some younger friends how she felt. "The book has everything to do with it," she thought, "as well as my heavenly and earthly Angels that surround me. The stories have such important messages, may they be healing ones." Then, she heard her Angels say "They will be." At that GiGi smiled.

Sara asked, "Are you OK? Are you sorry I invited her?"

"Oops, I'm sorry. I was just musing, didn't mean to be quiet. Definitely pleased she wants to come. What time do you want to feed us?" GiGi asked.

Sara responded, "Make it 6:30 to allow for the rest of her story. How about having sandwiches and salads?"

"It sounds good. I'll be there, on time with desert," said GiGi enthusiastically.

Later on, when GiGi arrived at Sara's she heard the usual greeting from Sara, calling out to her: "The door is open and welcome."

GiGi called back with "I'm on time and with the promised dessert."

Anita was already there and they greeted each other with a hug.

When Anita saw the ice cream, syrup and whipped cream, she smiled a big broad smile and said, "This reminds me of how my mother would allow me to have dessert first. I always felt so special and daring."

Sara laughed and said "Nothing will spoil if we want to be daring and have the yummy part first. How about you, GiGi?"

"I suspect we all thought our mothers were unique and wonderful when they did that. So let's continue the fun and eat away," GiGi replied.

And so they did.

Later, after finishing off the dessert with great satisfaction, Sara said "Well, it's time isn't it?"

GiGi answered with: "Well, we can eat our dinner if we're able."

"No, no," Sara said "I meant it's time for the rest of the story if Anita feels like it."

Anita said, "Yes, I'd like to finish and I hope you'll want it for the book." She settled back in her chair and began: "After the wedding we spent a lot of time visiting either my folks or Alan's and also at the girls' places as well. It was always family together. Alan's family that is, and always lots of booze. This was something new to me since my family never drank much except for wine and my father downing one whiskey with a funny facial expression. I used to ask him if he liked it and he would just laugh."

GiGi said, "Guess that was uncomfortable for you then wasn't it, all that booze?"

Anita nodded and said "Yes it certainly was."

GiGi felt fine asking her questions because Anita had invited questions. In fact, Anita had said many of the questions were ones she had asked herself thousands of times.

Anita continued her tale by saying, "Along with the whiskey came some pretty nasty remarks. Rose in particular, younger by two years than Sally, would make some remarks that made us all uncomfortable. Some of what she said was anti-Jewish but it was thinly veiled or just implied. Alan, after more than a few drinks, was pretty out of it. It was always Harold, Rose's husband, who would try to smooth things over. Of course Rose would sort of apologize in a hazy way – it was ghastly."

"Why did you even have anything to do with them?" asked Sara, innocently.

Anita said, "Harold would explain that she really didn't mean it.

Alan wouldn't even remember some of the talk."

"Did you ever get the strength to throw them out?" Sara asked.

"Sure, but that was years later when I finally gained my self-respect and wouldn't tolerate it anymore. I make no excuses for what I did or didn't do then," Anita declared, adding, "As I look back now and in talks with my many therapists, it was the only way I knew to survive."

GiGi looked at Anita and Sara and knowingly said, "Of course." Then with all the weight of 90 plus years of wisdom said, "Anita, you must forgive yourself for whatever you did or didn't do back then. Remember the times you were living in. It was a very different time and just be thankful you are here now and a stronger woman for having lived through that."

Anita looked at GiGi with tears welling up and simply said, "Thank you."

Sara, also teary, said nothing.

GiGi got up and said "It's time for a hug, I think." All three women stood up and fell into each other's embrace in a hug that went on for several moments. After the embrace they sat back down and collected themselves.

"So the question is would you want that abuse in the book?" asked Sara.

"You bet and how I was finally able to let them know my feelings, and how sorry I am for not being strong enough to help the children and myself," Anita said. "But that was then and we're here now and can't change the past."

Anita took a deep breath and then added, "I find it interesting that as a part of all this, Sally once told me confidentially that Rose had been very fond of someone before meeting Harold. She was pretty serious as was the fellow, but his mother broke it up because Rose wasn't Jewish. I did think that maybe Sally said it to sort of explain Rose but on the other hand, I knew that it happened a lot back then."

"Talk about irony," GiGi murmured. There was a brief pause then

GiGi asked, "In all this time did you ever think of not allowing the family to spend time with the children?"

"Of course not," Anita replied. "I may have felt like a victim but there was no way I would become a victimizer. I know it happens in lots of families but that doesn't make it right. The chain—that dreadful abusive chain – had to be broken at some point. What I did was limit the visits the children would have with them. They lived a distance from our home and that meant Alan had to drive back and forth. I stayed home and had solemn assurances from Sally that she would make sure that Alan drank nothing so he could drive safely."

"Did he not drink?" GiGi asked.

"No, I only found out when the children were grown that they were terrified by his driving home from those visits. I never knew – Sally had promised. I had said they could not go if Alan drank," Anita said.

"And the children never said anything to you after the trips?" Sara asked.

"Somehow I never suspected and as I think of it now, I wonder if I ever asked the children directly. In fact, thank you for bringing this up. As I remember, there was always a lot of 'Mom, look at my presents,' and 'See what I got,' and all that. But in all the excitement did I ever ask? I wonder now," Anita said trailing off a bit and looking as if she might cry again.

Suddenly Sara cleared her throat a bit. "Might this be a good time to stop and eat our dinner now?" she asked diplomatically. "This seems like a good time to take a break and you can think about all that another time."

GiGi and Anita agreed and all busied themselves with setting up the table.

As they began to eat, there was still a sort of unfinished feeling in the air—like Anita hadn't told something important. Then Anita broke the quiet with: "I want to share with you what happened to me last night."

After they finished their sandwiches, pickles and coleslaw, Anita started to tell them about her safe place.

GiGi and Sara tried to suppress their smiles. Sara hastened to assure Anita that she and GiGi had their own safe places and would share them another time.

"But first, GiGi said, "Sara, what about dessert?"

Sara went to the kitchen and brought out the empty ice cream box and all three burst out laughing. "Wherever they are our mothers are also laughing," Sara said.

Anita smiled at that and went back to telling about her safe place. She began by saying that hers was rather out of this world but most of the ones she heard about were also. She started with "I loved the seashore and had always hoped to see a mermaid. Obviously, she would become part of my safe place. She was the queen of all mermaids and had a small Angel mermaid on her shoulder called Tia. When I was troubled, I would visit her and she would clap her hands and her mermaid entourage would form a large circle around me. No sharks, no Orca, no creature could penetrate their circle. Tia was an Angel mermaid who would come to my shoulder to listen to my problems. She would reassure me that I was doing the best I could and there would always be better times. My biggest regret is that we didn't meet until I was 50 years old. Somehow, a wise friend suggested I pick a wild and wooly safe place and Tia must have been listening. She came to me first and then her mermaids. They have been my treasures ever since. Hopefully, I'll see my friends again tonight."

Little would GiGi and Sara know how their loving, listening presence for their new friend Anita had helped her. Later that night Anita found herself tossing and turning unable to get comfortable until she finally heard Tia whisper a suggestion in her ear. "Write a letter to yourself." That was a new one and needed a lot of thought. Anita promised herself to do it when she could. There was so much emotion around all this and she wasn't sure she could do it right away. But she knew it would be done when she was ready. She felt like she was talking to one of her friends, "You'll do it when you're ready." Well actually, she was since she was her own best friend.

Anita muttered, "Thank you Tia," as she fell asleep.

And so it was.

CHAPTER 18

DAVID FINALLY FINISHES
HIS STORY

It was a few days later when Sara and GiGi were again seated in the Rabbi's cozy study.

"I want to finish my story," said David. The women sat quietly waiting for him to continue. "What I didn't get to explain the other day, because of Kristy skinning her knee, was the reason Colleen was asking for a divorce. I was stunned but still able to muster some anger. I couldn't believe what I was hearing. I thought 'How the hell did we get from problems in the bedroom to a divorce?' I was livid. I began yelling I guess and Dr. Jameson tried to calm us both down as Colleen was beginning to shake from my angry outburst. It was then that the therapist told me there was someone else in Colleen's life and I really blew my stack. 'Who the hell is he?' I shouted in her face and Colleen looked horrified, got up and ran from the room."

David looked at Sara and GiGi who sat stunned across from him. He now realized his voice had been raised as he was reliving the story. As he looked at their startled expressions, he began to feel his face get red with embarrassment. "I'm sorry if I got a bit too animated. As you can see it was a very emotional time."

Sara and GiGi both nodded sympathetically at him.

David continued, "Anyway, the reason I think you may be interested in all this for the book is a letter that Colleen sent to me after that initial meeting in the therapist's office. I think perhaps if I read you the letter it will be easier for me to finish the story. May I read it to you now?"

"Please do," GiGi said with anticipation as she and Sara listened intently.

David,

There is so much I want to tell you, hopefully to help you understand what has happened to change me. Again, hopefully, you will be able to forgive me. Before I met you, in college there was one particular girl I was very attracted to. She felt the same way I did and we stayed with each other two times. At the same time, one of the girls took a picture of two other girls kissing and making out. Because of all the gossip — the harassment they endured — they became ill and had to leave school. My friend and I were terrified we would be discovered too and broke up our relationship. She moved to the West Coast after graduation and we never contacted each other again. After that, I only went out with boys but no one was interesting until I met you and fell madly in love. You were so special to me and still are. I still love you and wish it could be different for us.

To bring you up to date: While checking out Facebook one day, short-ly after Kristy's birth, I discovered my college friend and I contacted her. She was back in the area; we had lunch, and after a couple of meetings, discovered our old feelings for each other were still there. Believe me, I've tried to deny them, have been in therapy with Rita Jameson and it's no use. Georgie and I love each other and want to be together. She divorced her husband two years ago after discovering herself. I am asking you to divorce me. You and Kristy deserve someone different, a wife and mother in the so-called normal way.

I wrote to my sister, Kristen, who is just finishing nursing school, and she now knows the story. She is upset for all of us and wants you to know she will do anything to help with Kristy especially so my mom and dad will be able to see her as before. They adore her, are learning to love you, and I know will be shocked to hear my story. I don't know what their reaction will be. But that is something to face later. You, Kristy and

I are the important ones now and I hope we can make this as amenable as possible. Never thought to have to use that word with you, we have always been able to talk things over until now. Among my regrets is that we didn't have this conversation a long time ago. Rita Jameson suggested we talk face to face, but I couldn't until you knew the story. If you are willing to meet, I would be very grateful.

    Colleen

"So as you might imagine," David said, "My first reaction was I was extremely hurt and upset and all I could think to do was consult my attorney and get out of our marriage as quickly as possible. Even hurting Colleen and this other woman were part of my intense feelings at that moment. Complicating matters even more was the reaction of Colleen's parents."

David shifted uncomfortably again in his seat as he continued to tell his story. "Colleen's parents were extremely upset and very concerned about all of us but especially Kristy. They had heard how grandparents were not allowed to see their grandchildren after a divorce and were worried about that, as well as how they felt about Colleen. It was a difficult time for all, but when Colleen's sister Kristen was able to assure them I would never act that way they seemed able to accept the situation better."

David continued, "Well, as you may have guessed by now, Kristen and I met many times taking care of Kristy. Her nursing experience helped in hundreds of ways when Kristy was only 6 months old. Now that she is 5 she knows Kristen as her mother. Colleen had proposed naming her after her sister and I thought it was a pretty name too. Kristen and I became very good friends, and as time went by we fell in love and were married two years ago. My in-laws were thrilled of course and we have a good relationship now as the father of their grandchild. As it turned out Colleen's letter reminded me how much I loved her and that she didn't do this to hurt anyone, and that she still also loved me and our baby."

Sara and GiGi sat quietly as they realized how the letter had changed David's whole attitude. He continued, "The two of us did meet, tears and all and arranged for details of the divorce to be as simple as possible. We decided to wait to tell Kristy about her birth mom when she was a little older. We had advice on whether to wait or tell immediately and it was not an easy decision. Colleen planned to move to Oregon with Georgie on a five-year assignment so that made it a little easier and we agreed to make a statement with no blame to anyone."

Suddenly, GiGi felt extreme coldness enveloping her and looked over at Sara. She was extremely pale and kept shifting in her chair. David didn't seem to notice as he continued with his happy ending story. GiGi knew she had to do something and picking up her teacup, felt a slight tugging and spilled tea over her clothes.

"How careless of me," GiGi exclaimed, I'm so sorry but I think I better go home. Can we get all the good news another time and talk about the story for the book, David?"

David was all concerned for GiGi, still not noticing how pale Sara was. He agreed it would be better to continue later as Sara helped GiGi out of the chair. Saying their goodbyes, they moved swiftly towards the door.

Once they were in the elevator, Sara suggested they stop at her place and then broke into tears and said she didn't know how she could have kept silent any longer—a gay spouse, a mother leaving her baby and when was it best to tell about a birth mother. It was her story, her very own story, with different characters. She kept saying this was another sign to tell Sheila everything ASAP.

When they finished getting GiGi changed into a warm, cuddly blue robe, Sara kept hugging GiGi and repeating how her Angel GiGi had helped her one more time. GiGi said she couldn't take credit alone, she felt a tugging and that's how the tea was spilled. "Our Angels and I were looking out for you."

The two friends just sat quietly together for a while and after some time they said their goodbyes for the night and GiGi went home.

Sara sounded like she was in a much better place when she called the next day.

"Chrissie called all excited," said Sara, adding, "She thinks the trial of her uncle and brother will turn out better than she originally thought."

"Why would she think that?" GiGi inquired.

"Well, for one thing the Tarot cards said so."

"Sara, when did you do a reading?" GiGi asked. "She's in Florida."

"I know but she asked me to do one for her anyhow and sometimes it can work long distance too," Sara answered.

"What did you tell her?" GiGi was curious.

"Well in the reading, several of the most positive cards kept appearing. So when I shared that with her, we agreed that the outcome was promising," Sara said. "We couldn't possibly have known how much it would turn around, although the cards obviously knew."

GiGi was growing impatient for the real news and exclaimed, "So get on with it then, what happened?"

"Well it seems there was some trouble with their judge saying things in open court that weren't appropriate when the young women testified. Now he's in hot water. Apparently he told them they had encouraged the rapes and he suggested they'd better agree to some kind of deal if they hoped to get any sentence at all."

"That's terrible Sara. It sounds like the judge abused them verbally. And after going through all that physical abuse," GiGi declared. "Those poor young women."

"Yes and a complaint was made against the judge and Chrissie's not sure but she thinks they are going to bring him up on charges.

Wouldn't that be great?" Sara asked.

"Sure would be an example," GiGi said then added, "I know you reminded Chrissie to suggest these young women write letters to the rapists, even if they do it only for themselves."

"She told me they have been seeing a therapist and he suggested they write too," Sara said. "Hope the Angels and letters will help them to get over those brutal crimes but it might take a long time. There's a lot of work to be done to get over what they've gone through, in and out of court as well."

"I'm glad you heard from Chrissie about the court case," GiGi said. "How is she with her cancer treatment and how about her parents, are they still supportive?"

"She said that things were going well with both and, of course, she is very excited about the court stuff too. Especially since she had also been abused by her brother and uncle but couldn't testify because the statute of limitations had run out on the rape. Chrissie said at least now they will be properly punished," Sara recounted.

"We can all say thank goodness for that," GiGi said adding, "Glad she is doing so well and that the two young women are also getting some therapy. That should help a lot. And Sara I'm so glad it has lifted your spirits after our visit with David yesterday."

"Yes, sorry I put you in that uncomfortable position," Sara remarked, "But thanks to you and your Angels for rescuing me."

"Well, as long as we are talking about it, I should fill you in that David called me earlier. He wanted to check on how I was doing after the spilled tea incident," GiGi said.

"Oh? Do you think he suspected something?" Sara asked.

"No, he was just being sweet and checking up on an old lady who might have burned herself," GiGi answered. "He really is a very nice young man, who has been through a lot. In fact, as we were talking he asked again if I was really interested in the letter for the book. I assured him I was and that I needed the rest of the story as well. He suggested it was brief and could tell me right then if we both had time. I told him that I certainly did so he recounted the balance of his story."

"He did? What happened?" Sara asked, who sounded relieved.

"Well," GiGi recounted, "First of all David's mother, Naomi did get to meet and spend some time with her granddaughter Kristy and the Murphy family before she died. David said that made him and the Rabbi very happy. In addition, Colleen and her partner Georgie are returning to the area in a few weeks. This will give David and Colleen the chance to finally explain things to Kristy."

Sara let out a sigh of relief, "You and our Angels knew how emotional this whole story was for me. Thank you all for bringing me this happy ending."

The phone conversation ended with the usual loving words of friendship and some small talk and pleasantries of the kind longtime friends exchange with ease.

It was a couple of days later when Sara called with the words: "Safe place and more safe place and think of what might have happened."

GiGi immediately said, "Sara, you're not making sense and you're upset, concerned, whatever. Let's take a walk and then relax on our park bench. How does that sound?"

Sara readily agreed, even though it was a bit earlier than their usual time to go out. This must be important, GiGi thought and decided to bring some coffee and donuts and for their persistent pigeon friends, the usual dry bread.

When they were seated, Sara asked, "Do you remember talking about safe places the other day?"

GiGi answered, "Of course. Do you want to talk about it?"

"No. I want to talk about when I didn't have it, and my Nana and, oh a whole lot of other things, I guess," Sara answered.

"This sounds like true confessions to me, so start and I'll get the hankies ready," said GiGi, hoping to get a smile or something. No go. Sara just continued looking sad and even refused the coffee and donuts. This was definitely serious.

Sara started with: "You remember that Jonathan letter and how we both left home and were married. Well you know the gist of it. But you don't know what a wild teenager I was. In fact my mother asked Nana to take me on, hoping she would be able to control me. I didn't do drugs or sleep around, though my mother thought I did. I kept late hours, missed a lot of school and in general was a pretty obnoxious teenager. My mother and I just didn't, couldn't get along. We didn't talk to each other. It was usually a shouting match, then tears and it would start all over again."

GiGi exclaimed, "Sara, that's a 'you' I can hardly believe."

"Believe it," she said, "I'm not proud of it. Anyhow my Nana was so sweet and kind. I could go on and on. I was mean to her too. She was an absolute saint to put up with my shenanigans."

"So where does the safe place thing come into all this?" GiGi asked.

Sara said, "In that past, I do believe I might have been different with a safe place. Dear Lord, I surely needed something to help me survive. In fact, am not even sure I liked acting the way I did. I just did what my friends were doing. As I look back now, probably did my share of bullying as well. It was the thing to do and too bad if no one liked it."

GiGi asked, "Is that why you and Jonathan married? It was the thing to do?"

"Of course. Plus it got me away from my mother and Nana," Sara said.

"Oh Sara, what a terrible time you had. It's a wonder that you turned out so differently. However did you manage that?" GiGi asked.

"Well, when our marriage was such a disaster, I asked my favorite aunt, Maureen, if she could help me, Sara explained. She was a wise woman and accepted me even when I was bad. She just loved me and I loved her back. We had long talks and somehow she must have mentioned a safe place. It got me thinking. I remembered Muir Woods in California that the family had visited on vacation. At the time I pictured myself in the middle of those woods, with my fairy godmother protecting me from evil. I even named her Lady Samantha. Guess that was the TV program 'Bewitched' creeping into my thoughts."

"Why Sara," GiGi exclaimed, "Is that why you love looking at that picture in my bedroom. The one with the little girl in the woods with a huge Angel and all the little animals helping keep her safe?"

"Yes. That's the one," Sara said, adding "It had been in my heart for years but I never thought I could actually go there for protection. I then learned to imagine myself in those beautiful woods that had stood for ages. With my Angel and little animals, I didn't have to fight the world all the time. I could find some peace and survive in my safe place."

"Oh Sara," GiGi said with tears starting to gather behind eyes. "Your aunt must have been very special."

"Yes, she was and I'm forever grateful for that," Sara said. "Plus how she managed to help Nana and me. Nana and I were once again loving and helping each other until she died many years later."

"I love happy endings," GiGi said and Sara added, "Amen to that."

They sat and relaxed with their coffee and dessert in compatible silence—it definitely seemed like a brighter day.

And so it was.

CHAPTER 19

IT'S TIME FOR MOLLY'S WEDDING

Finally—the big day for Molly was almost here.

Sara would be driving with GiGi more than 100 miles for her niece's wedding the next day. They would be staying over two nights for her to visit with relatives.

"Her visiting, not my choice," GiGi was thinking.

GiGi had promised to go and was going to make the best of it.

As it would turn out, GiGi would do the visiting for Sara, who had other priorities.

Sara's little red car was stuffed with their clothes and essentials. They planned to arrive the day before the big day, as would Sybil and Sheila who were bridesmaids.

Sara took the scenic drive up, stopping several times for GiGi to walk and get unstuck, as she called it. Sara's car was comfortable on short trips, not on this longer one.

When they arrived at the hotel, GiGi was finally able to get to her room to relax. Sara decided to look for Sybil and Sheila and visit with whoever else had come early.

Again, plans were made to be broken. Sara returned to their room and announced that she had seen the same fellow she had met in Vermont ages ago. It turned out his name was Richard Lattimore and he was the groom's uncle.

"Uh Oh," thought GiGi, "There goes all that relative visiting—unless he's involved or something."

It turned out he was unattached, that is, until Sara arrived.

GiGi asked Sara if she had seen her sister Kate yet.

Sara replied "I doubt we'll see her till later. She'll be busy getting Molly and her bridesmaids organized. And if anyone can do a super job, it's my sis, Kate, especially for her daughter."

GiGi chuckled and thought how true. After all, she had a very successful wedding planner business.

GiGi reminded herself how she didn't want to accompany Sara to this one. She really was fond of Sara's family. She just hated any place with loud music and lots of strangers for two days and nights. "But maybe someone will have an interesting story for the book," she mused.

Sara brought her back to reality with "Are you dreaming, thinking of sleeping or what?"

GiGi knew she was expected to say something about this new man, Richard, and offer encouragement. GiGi feigned innocence with "Well, what are you waiting for? You're my favorite liaison and I need more stories for the book." She felt the Angels tugging and believed they were almost giggling.

Sara laughed and said, "You know me so well. I had already told Kate weeks ago, so you'll get at least one good story, after the wedding of course."

GiGi nodded and said, "Now I'm ready for a nap. See you later." She closed her eyes as Sara left the room.

GiGi had an hour to rest when Sybil and Sheila phoned. They expected to take her to lunch and bring her up to date on the relatives and friends they knew.

It seemed Molly had invited more than 500 people. At least it felt that way as the guests started arriving. GiGi discovered it was only 260 and Sybil and Sheila knew more than half of them. She met a few and promptly forgot their names, as she assumed they forgot hers too. Big smiles and happy nods were much easier.

GiGi and the girls decided to lunch on the terrace because it was such a beautiful day. As they were being seated, a small hand touched GiGi's arm. When GiGi turned she saw a young girl of maybe 7 or 8 years old. GiGi thought, "Now what is her name? Is it Gabrielle or Rebecca?"

At that moment Sybil asked, "Is everything alright Rebecca?"

"Ah," GiGi thought. "Rebecca, that was it."

Rebecca responded that she had a question for GiGi.

"Of course," said GiGi quickly and with a smile. "You can ask me anything you want. But remember, I may not always have the answer or want to share it."

Rebecca said, "OK. I want to know if you're writing a book. Can you answer that?"

GiGi immediately said, "Yes, I am and it's about bullies. Do you know any?"

Rebecca frowned and said, "I think so." Then she turned away quickly, blended in with the crowd and disappeared.

"Who and what was that all about?" asked GiGi.

Sheila said, "She's usually rather shy. Something must be bothering her that she even approached you. We'll check it out. She obviously didn't want to say more right then."

Sybil added, "She is such a dear. We'll find out why she's concerned and try to help." Then changing the subject Sybil said, "How about ordering lunch? I'm famished."

Just then the waitress came over with some menus and while Sybil, Sheila and GiGi looked over the delicious choices to make their selections, the girls started chattering on about their mom, Sara, and the man she met.

Sybil said, "I hope maybe she's onto something here. Who knows maybe she has finally found that soul mate she's always seeking."

The girls started to giggle and Sheila said, "I certainly hope so, he seems really nice. I think I like him. How about you, Sybil?"

"Yes I like him too. Maybe he's the one," Sybil said, turning to

GiGi. "What do you think?"

"I haven't actually met him yet so you'll have to wait for my two cents until after tonight," GiGi answered. "But right now it's time to give my two cents to the waitress on what delectable dish I've chosen. Before long you'll need to get me back to my room for a rest before tonight's festivities or I'll never be able to last."

Sybil said, "It's a deal." Sheila chimed in with "Oh we definitely want you to last."

So after the lunch, Sybil and Sheila got GiGi back to her room and went on their way for a while.

GiGi sighed, "Think I'll relax a bit before the big festivities – mmmm – this bed feels so good. Oops, I better review who is who tonight. Let's see, Sara did give me names on our drive up and their relative positions in the wedding party. Kate kept her married name – Taylor – for business. Her husband was killed in the first Gulf War. He was Samuel – middle name Keith, which he preferred. Samuel Keith Taylor. Kate was pregnant with Eric and Molly was two when he was killed."

GiGi tried to commit it all to memory but she needed notes to help out.

"So, Molly is marrying Mark Lattimore. Molly's brother, Eric, will be best man and the groom's sister, Diane, will be maid of honor," GiGi added to her notes. "Just make a big X," Sara suggested. "It's still up in the air whether Uncle John would escort Molly with her mom Kate."

GiGi continued to write thinking, "I hope Sara didn't notice I made notes. Let her think I have a wonderful memory."

GiGi went down the list, "Oh yes, the sisters, Sybil Gregory and Sheila Bennington, though I seldom use their last names. Then the ushers—oh I don't know—who cares. I'll never remember all the names when we meet. Thankfully there are only six attendants."

At that point the girls, Sybil and Sheila, came knocking, "Are you awake GiGi? We have news about Rebecca," Sybil said through the door. GiGi opened the door and invited them in.

"Why rest when there's a story or the potential of one?" GiGi thought.

They didn't have the whole story yet. Rebecca's family lived only a few miles from their town and it sounded like this would be continued when everyone got home. In any case, Rebecca's family had next door neighbors with whom they were very friendly. In fact, her mother and the boy next door's mother were partners in the same law firm.

Sheila and Sybil took turns filling in the story as they recounted it. It seemed what was troubling to Rebecca was that the boy, Jerry, was very mean to his dog. When no one was around, he would put the dog in her travel cage, place it in the backyard and pelt her with small rocks. Also he would throw stones at some cats and other small animals that sometimes lurked about their yards. One time Rebecca saw him kicking his dog until it cried. She was worried that he would do that to her pet dog and cat if he saw them outside and no one else was around. She wasn't sure how her mother would react because she liked Jerry and his family so much. Rebecca said she didn't know what to do. Then she told Sheila and Sybil that she overheard people talking about a book. She wondered if she could tell the lady who was writing it about Jerry and what he did and what she was afraid might happen.

GiGi was teary as she listened to the girls recount Rebecca's story. She said, "Oh that poor little one, to have to worry about that at her young age." Inside her heart, GiGi felt for all the children who had more, much more to worry about. "What a world!" she thought.

GiGi was glad to hear the girls tell how they were able to reassure Rebecca that it would be taken care of when they reached home. They had promised her they would make it all better and reported she seemed to be happier now that some "big people" knew the story she had been afraid to tell anyone.

Sara came into the room as the girls were leaving and suddenly there was some quiet.

GiGi needed to rest some more and was pleased when Sara said she wouldn't be coming back to their room tonight. After the reception, she was spending the night with Richard.

But first they both needed to rest before getting dressed. It was the perfect nap time and they were soon snoozing in their separate big beds.

Soon enough it was time for the wedding and everyone headed down for the ceremony and reception. Everything went smoothly according to plan and as a result everyone had a good time.

Later that night GiGi tried to relax after flopping into bed.

The wedding and reception had been huge successes. GiGi was exhausted from just watching the energetic dancing, loud music, the enormous servings and wonderful tasting food and the swarms of people. It sure was great to be able to snuggle in bed. Although she could still hear some music, she was in bed relaxing and fondly remembering the day.

It turned out that Uncle John did escort Molly with her mom Kate. The whole story was revealed when Sara found out the person who was supposed to sign for John was sick and unable to attend. She immediately volunteered, he felt more comfortable with his sister doing the signing and everyone was happy.

Molly looked beautiful in her gown. In fact all the attendants looked fabulous and the groom never stopped smiling, except to kiss his bride of course. It was a gay and happy day for all, even little Rebecca, as the sole flower girl, who managed a sort of wave to GiGi.

As far as GiGi knew, no one drank too much, or if they did they must have been politely escorted from the party. Kate ran a tight ship. No one was going to spoil this special day for her Molly and Mark.

GiGi looked forward to discussing more details with Sara and then recalled Sara had told her she planned to spend the whole evening with Richard and would see her next morning. "Hope she's found her soul mate," GiGi thought, adding, "If not—well, it was a lovely wedding and she did see many friends and relatives."

There was some tugging from her beloved Angels and GiGi realized she had better get some sleep. Tomorrow, if Kate was up to it, would be her story time.

As it turned out, Kate did have a story to share with GiGi.

Before long everyone was hugging and saying their goodbyes and heading home.

GiGi settled back in the car seat, looking forward to the long ride home quite unlike her thoughts about the ride coming up. The festivities were over, guests had returned to their homes and the happy couple was headed for a Bermuda honeymoon. There hadn't been too much tugging by her Angels, so GiGi must have remembered names. She was looking forward to returning home, even with the long car ride.

Kate had been able to take time for her story and wanted to get it into the book. Sara's dalliance with Richard had been interesting. Sybil and Sheila were on their way home too. All seemed well with her world. GiGi was anxious to finish the book. She felt it was ready or at least she was ready to complete the last few chapters.

Sara seemed ready for the long drive home too and the sharing of their impressions, as they called them. Sara was pleased she had spent the previous evening talking non-stop with Richard. They had a lot in common, but that spark she was looking for wasn't there, for him as well. If they had been right for each other, they both agreed two states' distance would not have mattered. As it was, they parted friends. She told GiGi he was a Veteran and Sara thought that he and Kate would have more in common. She would encourage Kate to somehow meet up with him.

GiGi said "There you go, being matchmaker again."

"I know and isn't it fun when it works out? I have a good feeling about them," Sara responded and GiGi had to agree. They both felt their Angels would clap their wings in agreement too.

Sara wanted to know how Kate felt about her late-husband, Keith, seeming to be there in spirit. A lot of the guests had known him and they talked freely about him and his little girl being married. Many also talked about what a fine job Kate had done raising the children.

GiGi said she had never met him, but definitely felt his spirit too.

"I'm glad Kate had that experience and also pleased she was able to finally tell the story after his death," said Sara, navigating carefully around a small cavalcade of cars that was moving very slowly.

"Nicely done" said GiGi, as Sara moved her car onto the highway.

"It looks like one of the cars is in trouble, hope it's not serious," Sara said as she settled back in her seat.

"I'm sure you know a lot of Kate's story," GiGi said "So if there's repetition, so be it."

Sara said, "Not really. Kate had talked about Keith's death, of course, but she told few details about why she wanted to leave the service. It was a tough time for her being pregnant with Eric and taking care of Molly."

"My impression is that she loved being in the service when Keith was still alive. Is that really so?" GiGi asked Sara.

"Oh yes and, even for a while, after he died. She had so many friends. The other service people were like her family. They were there for her and she was for them too when needed. That was how it was at the Army base where she and Keith had lived for more than five years," Sara explained.

GiGi recounted, "Kate shared that things were as OK as could be possible for a while. She was grateful for all the attention and help given her. She felt so vulnerable and talked about having the baby, under the care of the doctor she liked so much, and then returning to the States. She and Keith had been in the service together for so long. They had never planned to go back to civilian life so soon. In fact if they had to, they would only have moved back to be near you and the girls, Sara."

"Oh, I didn't know that. Hmm, then something must have happened that she moved near Keith's family when she left the service," Sara said.

"I think she felt the children needed grandparents who were still pretty active and they had begged her to come home to them. She felt it would have been a burden for you. You had your own problems. It worked out pretty well and they still weren't too far from you," GiGi related.

"Yeah, you're right. His family did a fabulous job. It's so sad his parents weren't able to attend. But I know Kate made special arrangement with the photographers to make an album just for them and they can share it with their friends at the assisted living community. Anyhow, a lot of Keith's family was there so they can report too." Then Sara looked thoughtful and said, "I know Kate missed not having Mom and Dad there too, just as John and I did. They are always missed on these special occasions."

GiGi asked Sara if they could stop for her to get unstuck and maybe they could check out the small restaurant as well. Sara was pleased at the suggestion as she was a bit stiff too. After all, they had plenty of time and no schedule that had to be strictly followed.

They relaxed with coffee ice cream cones as GiGi continued Kate's story. "Kate said she felt vulnerable and needy with Keith gone but she had lots of help. Then gradually, when some of Keith's buddies came to help they seemed to want a more intimate relationship. She wasn't sure at first but after a while it was clear when one of them would casually place his arm around her or just seemed to touch her in the wrong place. At first she would just shrug them away but sometimes it was pretty obvious. She had no one to talk this over with. In fact, two of her best girl friends were married to a couple of the guys who were the worst offenders. She felt she was being harassed when she was so vulnerable. They weren't like her husband's old pals. So she made plans to leave for the States. It took a lot of planning, and secrecy on her part. She used the excuse that Keith's family was urging her to come, so they could help with the baby's birth, etc. She would have to find another doctor for the birth and then for the children. She was finally able to complete her plans and left while just starting her seventh month. She knew she couldn't remain at the base any longer, despite her worry about leaving the doctor she liked and in whom she had such confidence."

GiGi quietly continued, "That took a lot of courage and luckily everything and everyone turned out fine."

"And I was in no shape to even try to help," Sara remarked. "Well, at least our mom produced two strong women, though at the time, we didn't feel that way."

"You better believe she did and she sure would be proud of you both. Well, I think we've time to just finish enjoying our cones and relax a bit before boarding our vehicle. What do you think, Sara?" asked GiGi.

Sara nodded agreement.

And so it was.

CHAPTER 20

IT'S NOW TIME TO FINISH THE BOOK

As they entered GiGi's apartment, GiGi and Sara both agreed that it was good to be home. Now it was time to finish the book. No more time out for anything—well, depending—like weddings, of course. They thanked their Angels for a safe journey and some tugging when it was necessary.

They both laughed as they realized their minds were in total, absolute agreement to finish the book. Then suddenly Sara began to chuckle and asked, "GiGi do you remember the times we had dreams about the book and each other. Your dream was about your wanting me to finish the book if you were not able to finish it. But here we are and you are finishing it and you're even thinking of a second book."

They both had a good laugh.

Sara continued, "Remember I called you and you were napping? and I said: 'I just had a dream. I fell asleep sitting at the computer. It was about your book in a bookstore window. It was in the center of dozens of other books, all brightly colored with different scenery and figures. Yours stood out with a special title. I asked if you wanted to guess what the title was? All you could mutter was 'I can't imagine and I want to go back to sleep.'"

Sara laughed and continued to recall the conversation adding "Then I said: 'OK, but first listen to the wonderful title. It was all lit up in bright gold neon bulbs. It said 'And So It Was' and underneath 'A Friendship Story.'"

GiGi began to laugh. "I remember saying 'You really don't want your name on that book, do you? It's because everyone would be pointing at you and saying she's the one, right?'"

Then GiGi continued "I also remember teasing you and asking 'What kind of title is that anyway – 'And So It Was'? What does it mean?'"

"And I told you 'Well, it means anything'," Sara replied. "I still feel that way. It makes you guess whether it's sad or happy, or whatever, depending on what you want."

"And I told you 'All I can say is what I said before'," GiGi remembered, "When it gets published, if another title is used, in my heart it will always be 'Sara, Our Angels and Me (A Friendship Story)'."

"Anyhow, you were right," Sara admitted, "I'll feel awkward if people ask 'Is that you?'"

GiGi smiled and said, "Remember what I told you then? Then think of it as you being an example of all our friends with their love, help and support. You can tell the other person: It's me and lots of others. And that should make them wonder, maybe they're in it too.'"

Sara also smiled and said, "And I responded 'Yeah, then they'll have to buy the book to find out, won't they?'"

GiGi remembered having said, "There you go – selling copies again. But now it's to work or our Angels will never stop tugging at us."

The friends hugged and laughed after reminiscing about their dreams. They made arrangements to do their final consulting after lunch the next day. The Angels had no need to remind them because the publishers' deadline was looming at the end of the week.

Later on when GiGi was working on the book she remembered how Sara became so involved in the book. She had asked Sara to give her opinion on the first two chapters. Gradually, Sara had become more involved and even started to do some editing and touching up as she called it. It just seemed to happen. GiGi never said anything except to thank her for her opinion and suggestions. She didn't want Sara to think she had any influence on the book's direction for fear Sara would want to stop helping since she always said "This is your book, GiGi." Without her realizing it, Sara became GiGi's editor and was a big part of getting the book published.

GiGi also remembered how she had worked in the writing class. A memoir of 90-plus years with all its traumas was something important to leave for her family. Then, when reading some chapters in class, the students and teacher agreed that a lot of people had similar bullying and abuse experiences. They encouraged her to tell hers and other people's stories, and to talk about how sent and unsent letters could be helpful. They were helping themselves too when they gave permission to include their stories in the book and even to talk about writing letters. One student offered to contribute her story and a long ago written letter.

GiGi also remembered how she had written dozens of chapters and needed some format, some organization to prepare for this different kind of book. She asked her friend Sara to just check them over and look where it was going now. GiGi sighed happily thinking "We are being published."

Sometime after that the first copies of the book arrived. Now it seemed there was more work to do to promote the book.

One day, weeks later, after the book was published, GiGi put her feet up on the hassock. "It sure is good to just relax my body from top to toes. And my hand needs rest even more after signing all those books. I think it was a successful book signing, don't you?" she asked Sara.

"I sure do. Look how many books sold. I told you the Fellowship would be a good place for your first signing. So many people care about what you're doing and were curious about the book you've been working on all these months. They know what a passion you've had to get out the information about bullying and when some people don't even realize it's happening to them. I heard a lot of nice remarks too. I especially like the one about how it will be easier to find safe places with earthly Angels now that there's a list of places and people to contact for help," remarked Sara.

"Yeah, I heard the same. I also heard from many people, who agreed with how our earthly Angels are there for us, we need only call on them. There were lots of remarks about how we're surrounded by Angels to protect us," GiGi said.

GiGi also said how helpful Sybil and Sheila had been. They had been extra hands and even ears when needed for when the crowds were crowding. They had no complaints about that. They all had a great time.

The girls were helping them review the day and contributing their own stories about the day's signing.

Sheila remarked on how many people asked Sara if she had all those things happen to her. Dozens also asked who some of the characters really were. Sara always told them yes and explained how we are all earthly Angels and reminded them to continue the good work. They would smile at her response and the moment would pass. The ones who had shared their stories and given permission to put them in the book also smiled; seemingly glad they could be part of it.

Sybil added her report about one of GiGi and Sara's acquaintances wanting to know why her story *wasn't* in the book. Sybil said, "I wonder how some of the other readers felt and maybe they bought the book to find out if they were in there."

They had a good chuckle thinking about how many people would be searching the book for hints of who each character was in GiGi's real life.

Ana called GiGi the next day, all excited. "Wait till you hear," she said out of breath. "The first … in the country … it's …"

"I agree that it sounds great," GiGi interrupted, then asked, "But by the way – what is it?" Ana laughed. "Oh right. You didn't see the paper. Well it's about the New Jersey State Legislature approving a new anti-bullying Bill of Rights. It is the very first in the country. Can you imagine?"

"I certainly can. That's wonderful news and about time, I must say," GiGi declared.

"I called Sara," Ana said, "To tell her that our school was discussing how to implement all this. Of course she said, 'It's about time too.' You know how she tried to curtail any bullying and harassment but wasn't always supported by the school administration. Plus the parents were something else."

GiGi asked, "What does that mean, good, bad or indifferent?"

"I guess it's a little bit of each, but mostly sort of indifferent. It was always very special when the parents or a single parent, in many cases, took things seriously and wanted to know how to help. Sometimes they thanked us as well. But Sara can tell you stories about some of them. She was more directly involved than me," Ana said.

"Mostly, as the school nurse, I might be the first to discover it when a student came to see me and it was obvious there was physical abuse. Too many times the victims would try to conceal it or make up some story or other," Ana explained, adding "You could always tell."

"What about emotional abuse?" asked GiGi.

"That was more in Sara's department. Uh-oh sorry to cut this short but I have to run. I just wanted to talk with you about this new law," Ana said.

"Oh Ana thanks so much for taking time to call. Hope to see you soon and by the way – your Victor is a dear," GiGi gushed.

"He is indeed. He told me about his visit and what he is doing. I'm so glad he is able to help. Well got to go, bye for now," Ana said.

The phone rang shortly after. When GiGi answered Sara asked, "Do you know how long I've waited for the politicians to finally discover how serious bullying and harassment are for anyone but particularly our young people? And how important it is to get the parents or parent immediately involved?"

"Well, thanks for the greeting," GiGi responded.

"Yes, it was rude but understandable with my excited bravos and huzzahs to New Jersey. May it be the first of many more states to follow," Sara said apologetically.

GiGi responded, "I'll say amen to that and forgive you. It was for a good cause."

Then Sara said, "Yes, knowing your next question, they did include electronic material as well. To quote: 'any gesture, any written, verbal or physical act or electronic communication whether single incident or series of incidents' and so on. I really believe that young woman's suicide triggered a huge outcry on top of all the other terrible incidents happening."

GiGi said, "Now the schools have to implement all this, don't they. Wonder how the different town school boards will handle it?"

"All we can do is wait and see. If not we can ask our Angels to tug at them. I wonder how do Angels react to bullies and tormentors," Sara pondered.

"I guess the same as always," said GiGi. "They would be accepting of them and then be tugging at them to help make them better people. In any case, the law will be doing most of it, don't you think?"

"True," Sara said. "Let's hope the Angels have some good influence like getting the victims to write letters to their bullies, even if they don't send them. As we know, it can help in healing from the bad experience."

"Yes, we know that. Let's hope the Angels can help them understand it too," GiGi affirmed.

"Help my old school's administrators too. They'll need it," Sara said. "Now they'll have to take things seriously, which they were re-luctant to do before."

GiGi said, "Of course they must it's the law!"

"A good law, too long in coming," Sara replied.

"So my final word for this talk is good for you and the law, my ad-vocate friend!" GiGi declared.

"Thanks to you as well. Bye for now," Sara replied.

A few days later, Ana called all excited again. She said the school now had a special program about bullying and she had been asked to talk at the assembly. A group of young people came to the school and acted out different kinds of bullying and that in turn started discussion groups among the students.

"Oh Ana, that sounds great and how are you involved?" GiGi asked.

"I'm telling about how victims often come to me as the school nurse and even many of the bullies come as well. That leads to more discussion about why they would come. There also are small groups with a facilitator to help make plans on how to stop this abuse," Ana explained.

"I'm sure this will bring about big changes in your school. Have you told Sara about all this? She'll be so pleased to know they're finally doing something," GiGi said.

"I called and left a message. She must be out gallivanting some-place and hopefully having a good time," Ana replied.

"I'm sure she'll be back to you ASAP for the good news," GiGi said.

They chatted for a few more minutes before hanging up. A few minutes later Ana called back.

"Is everything alright?" GiGi asked anxiously.

"Oh everything is fine. I just thought, how about you and Sara coming to school and telling about stories from your book. That could make it really dramatic," Ana said, adding, "You could mention how the letters have helped some people. Also, how one's friends become their Angels when helping."

GiGi responded, "I like the idea and I think Sara will agree. When is the program?"

"I'll keep you informed and now I really have to go," said Ana in a rushed voice.

And so it was.

CHAPTER 21

ALL THE ANTI-BULLYING WORK PAYS OFF

Several days later on a beautifully sunny day, GiGi sat at her kitchen window gazing at the clouds, guessing at the shapes and watching them change as they drifted by. She sipped her coffee and turned back to the computer. There it was, her "Invite" to the school show that evening.

Sara phoned at 11a.m., the clock was chiming. "I think you want to hear the chimes," GiGi said.

Sara agreed and said "I don't need my own chiming clock I can always call you when I want to hear them."

"Sure," GiGi said. "As long as it's a reasonable hour."

"I'll remember that," said Sara. "Reasonable is between 10 a.m. and 10 p.m., right?"

"Yeah and during all the chiming in between. You manage to time some of your calls on the half hour too," GiGi teased.

"OK. Enough of this chiming stuff," said Sara. "I want to talk about tonight."

GiGi said, "I think we have covered it pretty well by now."

"Well, be prepared when they announce that you started the whole idea talking about your book and that terrible story about Tina Scanlon committing suicide. How it prompted me to approach my old Junior High. How the teachers and administration agreed it would be a good idea to have a program about bullying," Sara warned.

"I only put the idea in your head," GiGi said, "You did all the work."

"Until you told me about Tina I never realized how serious it was," Sara reminded GiGi.

"But Sara, you saw some of it in your school," GiGi reminded her.

"True. But I thought they were just minor happenings. I didn't realize how serious they could be. Just like most of the other teachers and the administration," Sara admitted.

Ana had prepared GiGi for part of the evening. Ana had told GiGi they were planning to acknowledge Sara and asked her to keep it a secret. It seemed like it would be an interesting evening, GiGi thought.

What Ana didn't tell GiGi was that she would be a bigger part of the surprise than she thought.

Then Sara called to remind GiGi again that she would be picked up at 6:20 p.m. They didn't want to be late. The curtain went up 7 p.m. sharp.

Later when Sara arrived, GiGi said "I'm ready. Just don't go driving too fast."

Sara still drove 10 miles over the limit. She was determined not to be late. She parked in a spot that GiGi found helpful, not much walking.

Then came the greetings from the high school seniors who were monitoring the parking area: "Hi, Ms. Bennington." and "Good to see you Ms. Bennington." Most of them knew her from their days in junior high. Then the greetings from the teachers: "Hi Sara. We miss you!" and so on.

It went on for several minutes. Finally they were able to be escorted into the auditorium. It was like a royal procession as they were accompanied by honor roll students. Suddenly there was a drum roll. The students and teachers stood up. They were all wearing bright yellow t-shirts with the word "Bullying" and a large red "X" across it. Then, on signal they all turned and their shirt backs had: "Help the Tina Scanlon Scholarship Foundation" and listed below the bank's address where to send donations.

The audience chanted "Thank you, GiGi and Ms. Bennington" three times over as the two honored guests were presented with similar yellow t-shirts. GiGi and Sara reached for tissues. They noticed several other people doing the same. It was an emotional moment.

After the acknowledgment, the lights were dimmed. The show was about to begin.

Sara and GiGi had front row seats. As GiGi adjusted her ear phones and glasses she remarked: "They certainly know how to treat a lady."

Sara laughed and said, "It should always be so."

The students had done a fabulous job. The scenery must have taken a lot of time. They had divided the stage into two sections. One was for the student playing the victim. The other had several Internet screens and wiring. They were for the three girls and two boys who were playing the bullies.

They played their parts very well, interacting with each other, laughing and congratulating each other about the mean comments they posted about the victim. Then there was the victim's reaction showing how hurt she was. Then the victim finally spoke out firmly. She told them they would be reported. The bullies laughed and joked saying "So what?" and how no one could stop them.

At that, the school principal entered – the real principal – acting with them. He proceeded to tell them what could happen to bullies. He told them that bullying would not be tolerated. He explained why some people need to bully. He then said that some people need to be victims, or at least they think they do. There were many ways to deal with and help both kinds of people.

From the audience, there were shouts of "Right on!" and "You tell them."

The show was a huge success. The audience loved it, seeing the real principal acting with the students and taking bows with them. The crowd gave the actors five curtain calls. Then all the behind the scenes people were acknowledged.

Afterward, the principal thanked GiGi and Sara for starting the idea. He told GiGi how glad he was she had her book published because it was needed. He then told Sara he missed her too. GiGi knew Sara took great satisfaction in that. They had not always been in agreement.

Sara and GiGi left the auditorium carrying their t-shirts proudly. The shirts would be worn as often as possible. They were going to continue carrying the message. When Sara and GiGi heard all the positive remarks, they knew others would do the same. It had been a wonderfully successful evening.

Sara called the next day. She and GiGi talked about how excited the students had been. They agreed the performances were wonderful. It was great that the message was getting across.

"GiGi," Sara said, "A lot was due to you. I wouldn't have encouraged the teachers until you showed me those terrible newspaper reports."

"Yeah, you were all fired up, especially after another high school student committed suicide. You were determined to bring that story out in the open," GiGi said.

"I think everyone was fired up," Sara agreed. "When I suggested a program to the teachers, there was unanimous agreement."

"I know it took the students and teachers a lot of work to stage it," said GiGi. "And don't forget all the work you put in. You are supposed to be retired. You got in touch with Tina's parents, telling them you would help with the scholarship fund they had started in her memory."

"I feel very hopeful the students will long remember the message," Sara said. "And I know they are looking forward to seeing it mentioned on the TV and in the newspapers. With all the publicity, the public will remember it too."

The two friends spent a few minutes chatting over the previous day. It had been a good one. They agreed their Angels would have been pleased, as would Tina's Angels too.

Then Sara asked GiGi if she would consider thinking about

something else. She had a friend, Martha, who worked at her old school. She was impressed with GiGi, especially the reception she had received last night. Martha wanted to know if GiGi would talk with her daughter about GGs."

GiGi said, "I remember meeting Martha. Sure, I'll meet with them, though frankly I don't understand why."

"It's because her daughter's GG died a few months ago. Since then her daughter has been sad. She hasn't been her usual cheery self. They even had the doctor check her over. It's nothing physical. I think this is like the last resort. Martha didn't say that. I just feel it," Sara said.

"Is that your psychic powers?" GiGi asked. "Should I be flattered Martha wants me to try something, whatever that something may be?

"Yes you should be flattered. Martha teaches science. She also happens to be very serious. Not that teaching science makes her that way. It's her personality. I think you'll enjoy meeting her and her daughter. Plus, I know you'll like this, she's interested in the book," Sara declared.

"How could I refuse?" GiGi asked. "Give her my phone number. We can set up an appointment."

Suddenly GiGi heard the chimes. It was 11 a.m. She suggested to Sara they get to work.

She had mail she wanted to read, the pile of congratulations and other mail about the last successful book signing she had. They could share those another time.

Sara had plans for the scholarship fund. She wanted to contact more people and businesses as well. They'd have a lot to report at their next meeting. But for now, GiGi just wanted to take her time and read all the mail. It would be very special to be able to say: "Yes, I'm 92 years and feel like a youngster again. I've finished my dream book and you can do it too! Age makes no difference, it's the passion, knowledge of the subject and hard work that counts."

And so it was.

CHAPTER 22

GRACIE NEEDS A GG

It was Saturday; two days after Sara's request that GiGi meet with Martha and her daughter. "Hmm," GiGi thought, "I don't know her name or age."

The phone rang. It was Martha. The grandfather clock started its melodious 11 a.m. chiming. GiGi asked Martha to wait, or if she preferred, she could call her back.

Martha said, it was no problem. She loved to hear the chimes, as did her daughter Gracie.

When the chiming ceased they set their appointment for 1:30 p.m. at GiGi's place.

GiGi usually planned to meet at her apartment. They would be surrounded with Angels. The funny ones usually were ice breakers. The pretty ones were admired. Being allowed to hold them was always special for the children.

When the door knocking stopped, GiGi called out. "Welcome, the door's open."

Martha stepped into the living room holding Gracie's hand. GiGi remembered Martha. Her daughter was a miniature of her, with the same pretty blonde hair and lovely brown eyes. Both were dressed in soft green shorts and tops with green sneakers. They were a very pretty picture.

Then Gracie spotted the Angels on the walls and the venetian blinds. The shelves were loaded. She stepped away from Martha. She headed towards one of GiGi's favorites – the pearl Angel. GiGi said she could pick her up.

Gracie looked at Martha who said, "It's OK if GiGi says so." Soon

Gracie was wandering around the room. She carried the pearl Angel carefully. Finally she decided to sit on the footstool near GiGi's chair. She had questions – so did GiGi.

"My GG loved Angels too," Gracie said. "I miss her a lot. Why did she die?"

"Did she hurt a lot, Gracie?" asked GiGi.

"She never said. She didn't talk much then, not like before," Gracie said.

GiGi decided to ask more questions. "Was she at your birthday party? Which one was it?"

"It was 5 plus," Gracie answered, and she held up 5 fingers plus half a one from her other hand.

"Did your GG help you blow out the candles?" GiGi asked.

"Yeah and we had lots of ice cream and she gave me a big doll and lots of dolly clothes too," Gracie recalled.

"What's your dolly's name?" GiGi asked.

"I call her Peggy like my GG," Gracie answered.

"That's a beautiful name, Gracie. I think your GG likes it a lot," GiGi told the little girl.

"Yeah but we don't play together like we used to," Gracie said sadly.

"I know Gracie," GiGi said. "So I'd like to tell you a story. I'd like to tell you about the GG club. Did you ever hear of it?"

"No. Is it like Girl Scouts?" Gracie asked.

"Sort of," GiGi responded.

"OK," Gracie said, listening intently to every word GiGi said.

"Well, some GGs got together and decided they would form a club," GiGi began.

Gracie moved closer. When GiGi offered to share her chair, the little one climbed up.

"They lived near each other and every once in a while they would have a meeting," GiGi said, adding, "They wanted to be available for anyone who might need a GG, like you, Gracie."

"I do?" Gracie asked.

"Sure you do. Think of how you could play with Peggy and a GG," GiGi said.

Gracie tried to take all this in. She turned to Martha and asked "Could we play together like my GG?"

Martha assured her it would be OK.

They could tell stories to each other. They could play together. They could have ice cream cones at the local store. They could have fun. This seemed good to Gracie. She was relaxing. Then she asked "Would you be my GG?"

GiGi told her she could come over anytime. They would tell stories to the Angels. They could even rearrange them, if she wanted.

Gracie turned and gave her a big kiss. "I love you," Gracie said and ran over to Martha.

She gave Martha a big kiss. Martha mouthed "Thank you," and said they had to leave. They needed to go shopping.

Gracie said she wanted to stay and play.

Martha bent over and whispered in Gracie's ear. She must have said something magical because Gracie was now anxious to leave. It had something to do with a surprise, GiGi guessed, from the whispered conversation.

But before they left, they had to set up the next visit. After their various calendars were consulted, they set a date for two weeks. Gracie and Martha left after hugging and kissing GiGi again.

As they were leaving, GiGi wondered where the GG club idea came from. Was it her Angels? Maybe it went back years, how Sybil had called her GG. How they adopted each other on the spot. Whatever, she was glad it had happened. Martha had seemed pleased. Gracie had a GG to play with. GiGi had a Gracie to share with too.

As for Martha and Gracie, it was clear how happy this meeting made them both. Gracie went skipping down the hall to the elevator hardly able to control her excitement long enough to keep from spilling the surprise, as GiGi watched them head down the hallway waving goodbye. She thought it would be nice to invite a few young Fellowship children to a GG party. She wondered what special surprise Gracie would pick out for her. She knew that one of her special Angels would be just right. Martha would call as soon as the shopping was done. GiGi was certain Gracie would give her mom no peace until they were together again. It was nice to feel wanted by little ones.

"Let's see," GiGi thought. "We could meet in the library, pick out a book and I could read it to them. They could introduce their dolls or stuffed animal friends to each other and then have some ice cream and cookies. None of this may happen, of course. Little girls 5 and 6 have minds of their own. We'll see."

GiGi fell asleep that night still thinking about Gracie and all the fun things they could do together.

CHAPTER 23

SHEILA OVERHEARS SOMETHING SHE SHOULDN'T

Two days after her visit with Gracie, GiGi was trying to relax after having another talk with Sara about the whole Leila, Daniel and Sheila situation. She was reviewing in her mind the events of the past few weeks.

GiGi's book was published.

Sara had joined her for several successful book signings with many books sold.

GiGi was now beginning to think of the sequel. She even had a few chapters done and knew what she wanted for the next ones. This book would start out more organized with Sara's editing and organization. That is if Sara could concentrate with Sheila having the lint sightings more and more.

Sara was getting more anxious and she and GiGi were going over the story again to try and make some sense of the things Sheila was experiencing. In fact, GiGi and Sara had just hung up from their latest conversation about it.

Suddenly, there was a pounding on GiGi's door.

"GiGi, I need to speak with you now," shouted Sybil.

GiGi hurried to open the door and found Sybil, red faced with emotion, her arm lifted to pound again.

"I hope you don't intend to pound me as well," GiGi said, trying to get a smile but Sybil was too upset. "Sybil, come in and tell me what happened," GiGi said quietly, hoping to calm her down.

She and Sybil had a special relationship and Sybil had always been able to tell her anything and everything, even more than she could tell her own mother, Sara.

Starting to shake, Sybil sobbed out "I overheard you and Mom talking just a few minutes ago. I didn't mean to listen but suddenly I heard her say 'never really wanted Sheila' and then saying that's why it's so tough to explain."

GiGi was totally unprepared and just stood still in the entrance way. Suddenly she felt she had to sit down and grasped Sybil's arm and motioned towards a nearby chair.

Sybil looked at pale-faced GiGi and asked if she needed any meds. She became very concerned over GiGi's reaction and asked if she should call an ambulance.

GiGi insisted she was alright, just a bit unsteady and suggested making tea. Sybil hurriedly boiled the water and set out several tea bags and GiGi's special tea cups for both of them.

They sat down and waited for the water to boil. It seemed to take ages. Neither said anything until they were holding their hot tea cups.

Finally, GiGi broke the silence with "I know how you have always protected Sheila—you told her you were her big sister even when she was in your Mom's womb. It has always been that way for you. I know how concerned you were when that lint thing in the mirror started to happen more frequently."

"But what does all this mean, GiGi. I don't want to say anything to Mom that I overheard her—I wasn't trying to overhear—it just happened. Mom keeps reassuring Sheila about the lint thing but nothing changes."

Sybil continued, "Years ago, Sheila and I would cuddle in bed and she would wonder was her daddy really dead. Maybe he didn't want her. I would tell her how lucky we were to have our two daddies and by then I think Jon and Andy felt both of us were really their daughters. But now I question, is her father really dead or did he leave when she was born because he didn't want her like Mom said?"

GiGi took a deep breath and said firmly "I can say that Sheila was always wanted by her Mother and Father." Sybil seemed to relax just a little bit.

"Then what did Mom's statement mean?" Sybil asked.

"Sybil love I can't say anything more. Your Mom has to tell it."

"Then I'll go right over and ask her what it's all about. I don't want to upset Sheila. Those lint sightings are bad enough." Sybil was shaking again, sobbing and saying "How could Mom not tell Sheila if she knows something?"

"Sybil, please don't do that. Your Mother is extremely upset. I am talking to you as a friend but you will have to keep this confidential for now…and…"

Sybil interrupted her with "That's nonsense. What about Sheila being so upset?"

GiGi tried to explain that the whole story would be told but not right now. Sybil was not satisfied.

Sybil kept saying, "What about Sheila and now you are asking me not to mention anything to her?"

Concerned about how upset Sybil was getting and how upset Sheila was as well, GiGi asked Sybil if she would feel better if her boyfriend Robert was consulted.

"Why would I feel better about that? He's a detective not a mind reader," Sybil asked. "Are you thinking he might know a psychic the police department has successfully consulted? Right, he does know one that has helped find lost children and even two that were kidnapped."

Sybil continued, "Mom would have to tell him the whole story and Sheila too. I'm not comfortable about not telling her what someone knows and she doesn't. After all, she's the one who is most affected."

GiGi thought, "Oh dear one, if you only knew." Then said aloud, "I would like to explain this to your Mom before anything else is said or done. I can explain how you overheard her, not meaning to, and what we've discussed."

"Yeah, that would be better, GiGi. But you need to do it right away. I don't know how much longer Sheila can take this whole lint thing. She's beginning to think she's losing her mind," said Sybil, still not convinced this was the best way to go.

GiGi promised she would do it right away and keep in touch. They hugged and kissed and told each other that things had to get better.

After Sybil left, GiGi tried to think of the best way to tell Sara what happened. She was very concerned about Sara's reaction because she was in such a fragile state. "Oh Angels," GiGi thought, "I need you desperately and Sara needs you even more."

CHAPTER 24

SARA TELLS THE GIRLS EVERYTHING

The phone rang sharply interrupting GiGi's thoughts. It was Sara, speaking softly. "I just had a dream and..." Sara began to cry.

"Sara, what happened? Why are you crying? Are you all right?" GiGi asked with great concern in her voice.

"Oh GiGi it's too hard to talk now. Would you come over and..."

GiGi interrupted and said "I'll be right over. Don't do anything – I'll be right there."

GiGi hastily gathered her keys and cell phone, worrying that Sara might do something strange, and kept muttering "Angels watch over her," as she rushed to Sara's apartment.

When she arrived, the door was partially open and Sara was sitting on the floor rocking back and forth repeating "I'll do it, I'll do it, I'll do it," over and over and over.

GiGi helped her to the sofa, wrapped her in a handy shawl and just held her close saying "It's all right now," and trying to calm her.

GiGi gently held her friend as she rocked back and forth for a long time. After a while Sara's rocking slowed almost to a standstill and she just sat enveloped in the arms of her Angel, GiGi.

After another bit of time passed Sara slowly seemed to come back to herself, feeling safe that GiGi was with her. Finally Sara got out the words, "Thank you. I think I'm better now and would like some tea, if you wouldn't mind."

GiGi looked relieved and with a half-smile starting to come over her face, she hugged Sara tightly and said, "Whatever Madame wishes."

Trying hard to lighten the mood, GiGi added, "Think you can wait while your obedient servant makes some yummy relaxing tea?"

Sara smiled too, more like her old self and GiGi murmured, "Thank you Angels."

As they sipped their tea and started to relax a bit more, Sara started to tell GiGi her dream. She began by reminding GiGi about the story of her Nana. She talked about how Nana sometimes had psychic stories to tell Sara over the many years they were together after what Sara always referred to as her wild times.

GiGi nodded. She remembered the tales about Nana and how Sara said she loved those times. "But what does that have to do with your dream?" she asked.

"Well," Sara explained, "The dream had Nana in it. She kept telling me I had to tell the girls the whole story of Leila and little Daniel."

Sara continued, "Actually, she more than encouraged – she pushed me, in her Angel way, to tell the story. She said I would feel better to reveal the secret and then the girls and I could try to find the lost family."

Sara kept talking quietly but intently as GiGi just listened.

"Knowing how hard it would be," Sara said, "Nana made me promise to take this big step. 'Remember,' she said, 'You will finally find your very own son, as well as the girls their lost brother.' Nana could be most persuasive when alive and she was in the dream as well. It was like she was right here with me again. The whole dream was very eerie. It was so vivid and real. When I awoke I wasn't even sure it was a dream. That's why I needed your support as soon as possible, GiGi."

GiGi hugged Sara and said, "You have it always, whatever you do."

Sara shed a few tears and hugged GiGi back and said, "Thank you. I'll need your support more than ever for this. You know that."

GiGi asked, "When do you plan to see the girls?"

Sara answered, "I was going to ask you to invite them to your place as soon as possible. Perhaps you could tell them I am finally ready to explain – to share the family secret I've been keeping for so long."

GiGi replied, "Of course, dear Sara, whatever you wish. I am always here for you. Even though this seems like the hardest thing you'll ever do, I know you will get through this difficult undertaking."

GiGi was trying to help Sara relax and succeeded – somewhat – but both women were nervous about how things would turn out. There was an air of uncertainty surrounding the two old friends as they sat and sipped tea together.

After a short break and some more tea, GiGi took a deep breath, smiled a bit nervously at Sara, then picked up the phone and called, first Sybil, and then Sheila, who had just returned from her latest business trip to England. She told each of them that Sara had something very important to share with them, a family secret.

Both of the girls were anxious to know what it was. Sybil especially pressed GiGi to tell her right now on the phone or to put her mother on the phone. GiGi said, "Please Sybil, you know this is not that easy for your mom. Please be patient my dear sweet girl. All will be told soon enough."

Sybil reluctantly calmed down enough to set a time to come to GiGi's the next morning for the news her mother, Sara, needed to share.

Sheila was more inquisitive than pushy, asking, "GiGi, what is it? Is mom OK? She's not sick, is she?"

"Oh no dear Sheila, don't worry she's not sick," GiGi said aloud to Sheila, and then thought to herself, "Well not physically anyway, but surely heartsick. Hold her in your safe arms Angels!"

Both girls agreed to meet at GiGi's the next day at 9:30 a.m. They were most anxious and eager and assured GiGi they would be there at 9:30 a.m. sharp.

GiGi set the time early so Sara would have no chance to back away from this most important moment when she would finally share her secret with her daughters.

After the phone calls, GiGi hugged Sara and told her the arrangements had been made. They both teared up a bit and agreed this was definitely the right thing to do.

GiGi suggested Sara might want to go to bed early and maybe her Angel Nana would appear again. She was thinking that Angel Nana would push Sara again and not let her back away from telling the story. Sara laughed, a very small laugh, and said she had promised to do it and she would keep her promise. GiGi could relax and not worry. They kissed and promised to try to get a good rest and GiGi left, still more than a little nervous.

The next morning, Sheila and Sybil arrived right at 9:30 a.m. and were greeted with hugs and kisses by Sara, who had arrived much earlier, and GiGi who invited them to the living room and served up some of their favorite teas. The girls sat together on the sofa and GiGi took an armchair next to them. Sara said she preferred to stand and proceeded to move back and forth in front of them. Then she changed her mind and pulled another wing chair in front of the girls and took a cup of tea.

Sara put the cup down spilling a little as she was obviously very nervous. She looked at GiGi for support and then at the girls who sat immobile opposite her.

After a few moments, GiGi realized Sara wasn't sure how to tell her secret.

Should she just tell it right out or suggest they could ask questions as she told the story. Which was better for them and for her? As she started talking about Nana and her psychic abilities and then the dream, the format took its own shape. Sybil asked when Nana "came" to Sara. Sara said the previous night and then explained it was because of Sheila's seeing the lint in the mirror for all these months. "It seems a lot longer," Sheila muttered and asked Sara to explain the dream.

Sara repeated what Nana said in the dream, how many times seeing something in the mirror that wasn't really there, meant someone
was looking for you. Sara said perhaps she'd better start from the beginning and explain the secret and all would become clear to them.
At that, the girls both settled back on the sofa and waited with quiet
intensity for the story.

Sara told them all about her friends, Leila and Daniel, the wedding
she helped them plan and then Daniel's unexpected death in a serious
auto accident more than 30 years ago. Sara told of how Leila had tried
to become pregnant but was never able to carry the fetus to full term.
She explained how Leila then insisted on Daniel storing some sperm
and they would try again in the future. But then Daniel was gone so
suddenly. Leila was still intent on having a little boy just like Daniel,
especially after losing him. It was almost an obsession with her, Sara
recalled. Since they had stored his sperm it was actually possible to do
it and that made Leila even more intent on making it happen.

After a few months of wearing her down, Leila convinced Sara to
agree to be a surrogate mother so Leila could have her little Daniel.
Leila offered to help Sara financially since she knew that many times,
the single mom needed assistance and was too proud to ask for it.
After much soul-searching, Sara reluctantly did agree and gave birth 9
months later to a pair of healthy twins. The hospital records mistaken-
ly showed Leila as the boy's mother and Sara as the girl's mother. It was
an accidental thing but to Leila it was a miracle since she really only
wanted the boy. She insisted on Sara keeping the little girl and again
offered financial assistance. Sara agreed since the twins were actually
both hers and Daniel's. Leila had insisted on that remaining a secret so
no one would know little Daniel was from Sara's eggs and not hers.
Leila believed the boy would look so much like her late husband that
no one would know he wasn't her son too. But she feared that a girl
would look too much like Sara and that was something Leila couldn't
bear.

Sara knew that Leila could well afford the additional money since she had been privy to Daniel's wealth when planning the wedding. Leila also promised to be involved as they became older. She said they would always be friends and keep in touch.

Sadly, Leila never kept her promise and secretly left the area as soon as she could. Both little Daniel and little Sheila were very young the last time they saw each other and Sara saw her son.

As the girls sat transfixed listening to the story, Sara made sure to explain that she had grown so attached to the baby during the pregnancy that she often thought it might be too hard to give the baby up to Leila. So when Sheila came along as part of the package Sara was more than ecstatic at the prospect of having another little girl to raise and it certainly made it easier not to have to explain to Sybil where the baby went, when Sybil had also been bonding with the child Sara had been carrying.

"Sybil," Sara said directly to her older daughter, "You had also grown attached and would pat my tummy and tell your little sister how you would take care of her. It was heart-wrenching for me at times because I thought at the time it was just a little boy and that soon I would have to tell you the baby was gone. The prospect of that weighed so heavily on me that when Sheila was born it was a very easy decision to keep her. It was a relief really. Of course we would keep her. It was meant to be. I am sure the Angels worked overtime on that one."

The girls just sat stunned for a few moments. Then suddenly Sybil jumped up and rushed from the room yelling at Sara, "How could you?! How selfish of you not to tell Sheila who she really is. Not to tell me the truth. I hate you for keeping such a terrible secret from us both!!"

Sheila quickly followed after her big sister and tried to put her arms around her saying, "It's all right Sybil. I'm OK. It all makes some sense now. I can handle this big sister. I can."

Sheila got Sybil to sit down and stop crying long enough to listen to what Sheila had to say on the subject. After all it was her life they were talking about.

"Sybil, I'm not crazy," Sheila said. "The lint doesn't mean that I'm crazy it means I have a brother and he's looking for me if what Nana said in mom's dream is really true."

Sheila quickly added, "It means you have a brother too. Think of it, we have a bigger family than we thought, even if we don't know where he is. Maybe he has a wife and kids by now too. Please, please for my sake try to feel that Mom was doing the right thing for all of us at the time. She was about our age, a single mother, going to school and working, taking care of you, a 2-year-old, and me a newborn. You have to agree that she did a good job with and for us."

Sybil was still looking upset and angry but she was trying to listen to her sister and take it all in without exploding again.

Sheila could see that Sybil was trying but was struggling so she began to tell her a story.

"You know on my recent business trip to England something happened that I think might be helpful. I was at the fair enjoying the day when I came upon a sweet little girl who was crying because she got separated from her parents and brother. She was lost and was feeling frightened and I asked her what was wrong. She told me and I said, 'Do you believe in Angels, little one?' She said she did and I said, 'Well think of me as your own personal guardian Angel. I will get you back to your folks, I promise.' She said she would believe in me because I reminded her of her daddy. I guess he told her stories about Angels too, I don't know. Anyway I walked around with her until suddenly she squealed with delight and ran from my side to where she saw her brother and mom. It was such an amazing moment."

Sybil listened to her sister's story and then said, "What has that got to do with anything?"

Sheila said, "You're forgetting that the little baby boy we have been told about today is not just our brother, Sybil, he's Mom's child, her only son. Imagine how she will feel, much like that mother I reunited with the little girl, I would imagine. That mother scooped the little girl up and was crying such tears of relief that I just walked away without saying another word. I just left them to their celebration. It was so touching I walked away weeping to myself. Can you think how much mom's heart has been broken over this boy, now a man? Think about that before you express anymore anger toward Mom over this."

Sheila hugged her sister tightly and said into her ear, "Please, please go to her. That little Daniel is her very own son. Think of how she must feel."

Sybil broke down and cried into her sister's shoulder as they hugged for several minutes. Then when Sybil seemed ready they headed back to the other room where GiGi was hugging Sara as they both wept and waited for the girls to return.

As Sheila and Sybil came back into the living room, GiGi moved from hugging and consoling Sara to hugging them and saying she loved them and hoped they could understand Sara's actions those many years ago.

"No excuses, just reasons," GiGi said softly as she slowly moved Sara and the girls closer together and helped them sit together on the sofa.

Sybil sobbed out through tears, "Mom I am sorry. I wasn't thinking about how hard this must have been for you."

Sara smiled a little smile as she grabbed Sybil and said, "It's all right, honey."

GiGi smiled at that and made a bow to the three of them and said she had a suggestion to make. Placing a box of tissues between the three as they settled on the couch in front of her, GiGi said, "This has been such an emotional day and there are still so many questions and answers to be addressed why don't the three of you take some time to think and plan how you will work together to find Daniel and bring him back into your – our – family?"

The three of them nodded eagerly, realizing they needed time to try to absorb all of what had happened. They needed time to become close again. They definitely needed time.

As they sat there thinking, Sybil said, "Well there's nothing else to do but try to find Daniel."

Sara said, "I hate to say this but I have tried from time to time to find him but Leila kept moving them around the world and marrying and divorcing all these different men. I haven't ever had any luck so far, girls. I'm so sorry to say."

"Look Mom," Sheila said, "The good news from finally sharing this with us – hard as it was – is that now you are not alone in the search. You've got GiGi, Sybil and Robert – my future brother-in-law the detective – and me, a journalist, to help you."

Sybil said she would call Robert right away and put him on Daniel's trail.

Then GiGi said, "This can be our next book Sara – "Finding Daniel."

Sara said, "Uh-oh here we go again. We just finished your last book and now you are pulling me into another book. I knew you'd sneak that in somehow."

GiGi's eyes twinkled as she said with feigned innocence, "I don't know what you mean about sneaking it in, I have always said you were needed to help me with the next book. After all you are my ears, remember?"

Sara and the girls all laughed along with GiGi and then Sara looked at all three of the women in her life and said, "Thank you my three Angels."

And so it was.

CPSIA information can be obtained at www.ICGtesting.com
Printed in the USA
BVOW07s1519210813

329107BV00001B/5/P